Wilfrid Chateauclair

The Young Seigneur

Nation-Making

Wilfrid Chateauclair

The Young Seigneur
Nation-Making

ISBN/EAN: 9783743407848

Manufactured in Europe, USA, Canada, Australia, Japa

Cover: Foto ©Andreas Hilbeck / pixelio.de

Manufactured and distributed by brebook publishing software (www.brebook.com)

Wilfrid Chateauclair

The Young Seigneur

THE YOUNG SEIGNEUR;

OR,

NATION-MAKING.

BY

WILFRID CHÂTEAUCLAIR.

MONTREAL:

WM. DRYSDALE & CO., PUBLISHERS, 232 ST. JAMES STREET.

1888.

PREFACE.

The chief aim of this book is the perhaps too bold one—*to map out a future for the Canadian nation,* which has been hitherto drifting without any plan.

A lesser purpose of it is to make some of the atmosphere of French Canada understood by those who speak English. The writer hopes to have done some service to these brothers of ours in using as his hero one of those lofty characters which their circle has produced more than once.

The book is not a political work. It must by no means be taken for a Grit diatribe. The writer is an old-fashioned Tory and an old-fashioned Liberal : all his parties are dead, and he is at present in a universal Opposition. The party names he uses are, therefore, in any present-day application, simply typical, and the work is not a political one in any current sense.

There are those who will say his characters are untrue and impossible. To these he would answer : Everything here, apart from a few little inaccuracies, is studied from the life, and you can find item, man and date for the essential particulars.

A charge of Metaphysics will be advanced also, by a generation not too willing to think. *Mon ami,* what we give you of that is not very hard. If you cannot understand it, leave it out or study Emerson. The main subject of the book cannot be treated otherwise than with an attempt to ground it deeply.

If Bigotry may not impossibly be laid to the author by some, because he has drawn two or three of the characters from unusual quarters and described them freely ; the many who know him will limit any phrases to the several characters as individuals.

Lastly, the book is not a novel. It consequently escapes the awful charge of being 'a novel with a purpose.' None can feel more conscious of its imperfections than the writer, or will regret more if it treads on any sensitive toes.

WILFRID CHÂTEAUCLAIR.

Dormillière, March, 1888.

TABLE OF CONTENTS.

BOOK I.

BOOK II.

BOOK I.

THE YOUNG SEIGNEUR.

CHAPTER I.

THE MANOIR OF DORMILLIÈRE.

In the year One Thousand Eight Hundred and Seventy odd, about six years after the confederation of the Provinces into the Dominion of Canada, an Ontarian went down into Quebec,—an event then almost as rare as a Quebecker entering Ontario.

"It's a queer old Province, and romantic to me," said the Montrealer with whom old Mr. Chrysler (the Ontarian) fell in on the steamer descending to Sorel, and who had been giving him the names of the villages they passed in the broad and verdant panorama of the shores of the St. Lawrence.

In truth, it *is* a queer, romantic Province, that ancient Province of Quebec,—ancient in store of heroic and picturesque memories, though the three centuries of its history would look foreshortened to people of Europe, and Canada herself is not yet alive to the far-reaching import of each deed and journey of the chevaliers of its early days.

Here, a hundred and thirty years after the Conquest, a million and a half of Normans and Bretons, speaking the language of France and preserving her institutions, still people the shores of the River and the Gulf. Their white cottages dot the banks like an endless string of pearls, their willows shade the hamlets and lean over the courses of brooks, their tapering parish spires nestle in the landscape of their new-world *patrie.*

"What is that?" exclaimed the Ontarian, suddenly, lifting his hand, his eyes brightening with an interest unwonted for a man beyond middle age.

The steamer was passing close to the shore, making for a pier some distance ahead ; and, surmounting the high bank, a majestic scene arose, facing them like an apparition. It was a grey Tudor mansion of weather-stained stone, with churchy pinnacles, a strange-looking bright tin roof, and, towering around the sides and back of its grounds a lofty walk of pine trees, marshalled in dark, square, overshadowing array, out of which, as if surrounded by a guard of powerful forest spirits, the mansion looked forth like a resuscitated Elizabethan reality. Its mien seemed to say : " I am not of yesterday, and shall pass tranquilly on into the centuries to come : old traditions cluster quietly about my gables ; and rest is here."

"That is the Manoir of Dormillière," replied the Montrealer, as the steamer, whose paddles had stopped their roar, glided silently by.

Impressive was the Manoir, with its cool shades and air of erect lordliness, its solemn grey walls and pinnacled gables, the beautiful depressed arch of its front door; and its dream-like foreground of river mirroring its majestic guard of pines.

"I knew," said Chrysler, "that you had your seigniories in Quebec, and some sort of a feudal history, far back, but I never dreamed of such seats."

" O, the Seigneurs * have not yet altogether disappeared," returned the Montrealer. " Twenty years ago their position was feudal enough to be considered oppressive ; and here and there still, over the Province, in some grove of pines or elms, or at some picturesque bend of

---

* The old French gentry or *noblesse.*

a river, or in the shelter of some wooded hill beside the sea, the old-fashioned residence is to be descried, seated in its broad *demesne* with trees, gardens and capacious buildings about it, and at no great distance an old round windmill."

" Who lives in this one ?"

" The Havilands. An English name but considered French ;— grandfather an officer, an English captain, who married the heiress of the old D'Argentenayes, of this place."

" Mr. Haviland is the name of the person I am going to visit."

" The M. P. ?"

" Yes, he is an M. P."

" A fine young fellow, then. His first name is Chamilly. His father was a queer man—the Honorable Chateauguay—perhaps you've heard of *him ?* He was of a sort of an antiquarian and genealogical turn, you know, and made a hobby of preserving old civilities and traditions, so that Dormillière is said to be somewhat of a rum place."

The Ontarian thanked his acquaintance and got ready for landing at the pier.

CHAPTER II.

THE YOUNG SEIGNEUR.

A young man stepped forward and greeted him heartily. It was the "Chamilly" Haviland of whom they had been speaking.

Mr. Chrysler and he were members together of the Dominion Parliament and the present visit was the outcome of a special purpose. "It is a pity the rest of the country does not know my people more closely," Haviland wrote in his invitation :—"If you will do my house the honor of your presence, I am sure there is much of their life to which we could introduce you."

"I am delighted you arrive at this time;" he exclaimed. "My election is coming." And he talked cheerfully and busied himself making the visitor comfortable in his drag.

As luck will have it, the enactment of one of the old local customs occurs as they sit waiting for room to drive off the pier. The rustic gathering of Lower-Canadian *habitants* who are crowding it with their native ponies and hay-carts and their stuff-coated, deliberate persons, is beginning to break apart as the steamer swings heavily away. The pedestrians are already stringing off along the road and each jaunty Telesphore and Jacques, the driver of a horse, leaps jovially into his cart ; but all the carts are halting a moment by some curious common accord. Why is this ?

Suddenly a loud voice shouts :

"MALBROUCK IS DEAD !"

A pause follows.

"*It is not true,*" one forcibly contradicts.

"Yes, he is dead !" reiterates the first.

"It is not true ! " insists the other.

"He is dead and in his bier ! "

The second is incredulous :

"You but tell me that to jeer ? "

But the crowd who have been smiling gleefully over the proceedings, affect to resign themselves to the bad news of Malbrouck's death, and all altogether groan in hoarse bass mockery :

"ÇA VA MA-A-A-L ! !" *

Every one immediately dashes off in all haste, whips crack, wheels fly, and shouting, racing and singing along all the roads, the countryfolk rattle away to their homes. Our two turn their wheels towards the Manor-house, gleefully amused.

"Who is Malbrouck ? " Chrysler enquired.

"Marlborough. That must have been originally enacted in the French camps that fought him in Flanders. I fancy the soldiers of Montcalm shouting it at night among their tents here as they held the country against the English."

They drove along looking about the country and conversing. Chrysler breathed in the fresh draughts which swept across the wide stretches of river-view that lay open in bird-like perspective from the crest of the terraces on which the Dormillière *côte*, or countryside, was perched, and along which the road ran.

"Come up, my little buds ! " the young man cried in French, to a pair of baby girls who, holding each others' hands, were crowding on the edge of the ditch-weeds, out of the wheels' way.

"Houp-la ! " he cried, helping the laughing little things up one after the other by their hands, and then whipping forward. " How

---
* That is bad !

much are you going to give me for this? Do you think we drive people for nothing, eh?" The children nestled themselves down with beaming faces. "Tell me, *bidoux*," * he laughed again, "What are you going to give me?"

Both hung their heads. One of them quickly threw her arms up around his neck and, kissing him, said, "I will pay you this way," and the other began to follow suit.

"Stop, stop, my dears. You must not stifle your seigneur," he cried in the highest glee, returning their embraces.

One of our poets claims that there is something of earthliness in the kisses of all but children :—

> "But in a little child's warm kiss
> Is naught but heaven above,
> So sweet it is, so pure it is,
> So full of faith and love."

So it seemed to Chrysler as he saw this first of the relations between the young Seigneur and his people.

---

* Bidoux is a term of endearment for children.

CHAPTER III.

HAVILAND'S IDEA.

"GRAND MASTER.—O, if you knew what our astrologers say of the coming age and of our age, that has in it more history within a hundred years than all the world had in four thousand years before."—CAMPANELLA—*The City of the Sun.*

When they arrived before the Manor House front, Mr. Chrysler could almost believe himself in some ancestral place in Europe, the pinnacles clustered with such a tranquil grace and the walk of pines surrounding the place seemed to frown with such cool, dark shades.

Within, he found it a comfortable mingling of ancient family portraits and hanging swords strung around the walls, elaborate, ornate old mantel ornaments, an immense carved fireplace, and such modern conveniences as Eastlake Cabinets, student's lamps and electric bell. In a distant corner of the large united dining and drawing-room, the evidently favorite object was a full-size cast of the Apollo Belvedere.

Chamilly introduced him respectfully to his grandmother, Madame Bois-Hébert, an aged, quiet lady, with dark eyes.

In the expressive face of the young man could be traced a resemblance to hers, and the grace of form and movement which his firmer limbs and greater activity gave him, were evidently something like what the dignity of mien and carriage that were still left her by age had once been.

He was tall and had a handsome make, and kindly, generous face. The features of his countenance were marked ones, denoting clear intelligent opinions; and his hair, moustache and young beard, all of jet black, contrasted well with the color which enriched his brunet cheek. Whether it was due to a happy chance or to the surroundings of his life, or whether descent from superior races has something in it, existence had been generous to him in attractions.

When Madame withdrew, after the tea, he gave Mr. Chrysler a chair by the fireplace in the drawing-room end of the apartment, for it was a cool evening, and saying :—" Do you mind this ? It is a liking of mine," stepped over to the lamps and turned them down, throwing the light of the burning wood upon the pictures and *objets d'art* which adorned the apartment.

The great cast of Apollo, though in shadow, stood out against a back-ground of deep red hangings in its corner and attracted the older gentleman's remarks.

"I have arranged the surroundings to recall my first impression of him in the Vatican Galleries," said the other. "I was wandering among that riches of fine statues and had begun to feel it an *embarras*, as our own phrase goes, when I came into a chamber and saw in the midst of it this most beautiful of the deities rising lightly before me, looking ahead after the arrow he has shot."

" You have been in Italy, then ?"

" I have, Sir," he answered, "I have had my Italian days like Longfellow ;" and, looking into the fire, he continued low, almost to himself :—

> " ..... Land of the Madonna :
> How beautiful it is ! It seems a garden
> Of Paradise ..... Long years ago
> I wandered as a youth among its bowers
> And never from my heart has faded quite
> Its memory, that like a summer sunset,
> Encircles with a ring of purple light
> All the horizon of my youth."

As Chrysler regarded him then and heard this free expression of feeling he could not but feel that Haviland was a foreigner, different from the British peoples.

"And yet," mused Haviland, in a moment again, "Have we not a more than Italy in this beautiful country of our own ?"

After weighing his companion in thought for a few moments longer, according to a habit of his, the elder man recollected another matter :—

"You have resigned your seat in the Dominion House to enter the Provincial. Why is that ?"

"A new turn has arrived in affairs, sir. The Honorable Genest's fever has broken him down. He cannot fill a place where activity is needed. Until the fever, he was an influence, you know, in the Dominion House, while I was in the Local. After it, he arranged that we should exchange seats, as the Legislature has latterly been so quiet. Lately, however, Picault's corruptionists, whom we thought crushed, have made another assault for the moneys, bullied, lied, and bribed, weighed their silver to the Iscariots, and edged Genest out of his seat."

"Who is their man here ?"

"Libergent, lawyer. The election was annulled for frauds, but by moving the heavens and earth of the Courts they saved Libergent from disqualification, and now he appears again against us. Our cause calls for energetic action in the Legislature, so Genest and I are changing places back again."

"I hope you will not be lost to us long ?"

"No longer than I can help. The national work will never cease to attract me. *Is it not sublime this nation-making ?*—that this generation, and particularly a few individuals like you, sir, and myself should be honored by Heaven with the task of founding a people ! It is as grand as the nebulous making of stars ! "

The seigneur's manner was full of enthusiasm.

"I can't see it as you young men do," Chrysler said, in an inflection suggestive of regret. "What may we effect beyond trying
to keep Government pure and prudent, and we are often powerless to
do even that? Nor can we form the future character of the people
much, but must leave that to themselves, don't you think?"

"A partial truth," he returned, meditatively,—"a great one too.
When I go into the country among the farmers, I often think : 'The
people are the true nation-makers.'"

"And Providence has apparently designed it," the old man proceeded in his gentle strain, "to be our modest lot to follow the lead
of other lands more developed and better situated. Where do you
discover anything striking in the outlook?"

"I do not care for a thing because it is striking ; but I care for a
great thing if it is really great. Do not think me too daring if I
suggest for a moment that Canada should aim to lead the nations
instead of being led. I believe that she can do it, if she only has
enough persistence. A people should plan for a thousand years and
be willing to wait centuries. Still, merely to lead is very subordinate
in my view : a nation should only exist, and will only exist per-
manently, if it has a *reason of existence*. France has hers in the needs
of the inhabitants of a vast plain ; local Britain in those of an island ;
with Israel it was religion ; with Imperial Rome, organised civilization ; Panhellenism had the mission of intellect ; Canada too, to exist,
must have a good reason why her people shall live and act together."

"What then is our 'reason of existence?'"

"It must be an *aim*, a *work*," he said soberly."

The elder man was surprised. "My dear Haviland," he exclaimed,
"Are you sure you are practical?"

"I think I am practical, Mr. Chrysler," Haviland replied firmly.
"I have that objection so thoroughly in mind, that I would not expose
my news to an ordinary man. It is because you are broad, liberal

and willing to examine matters in a large aspect, and that I think
that in a large aspect I shall be justified, as at least not unreasonable,
that I open my heart to you. Believe me, I am not unpractical, but
only seeking a higher plane of practicality."

"But how do you propose to get the people to follow this aim?"

"If they were shown a sensible reason why they *ought* to be a
nation," said he with calm distinctness,—"a reason more simple and
great than any that could be advanced against it—it is all they would
require. I propose a clear ideal for them—a vision of what Canada ought
to be and do; towards which they can look, and feel that every move
of progress adds a definite stage to a definite and really worthy edifice."

"The-oretical" Chrysler murmured slowly, shaking his head.

"For a man, but not for a People!" the young Member cried.

Both were silent some moments. The elder looked up at last.
"What sort of Ideal would you offer them?"

"Simply Ideal Canada, and the vista of her proper national work,
the highest she might be, and the best she might perform, situated as
she is, all time being given and the utmost stretch of aims. As
Plato's mind's eye saw his Republic, Bacon his New Atlantis,
More his Utopia; so let us see before and above us the Ideal Canada,
and boldly aim at the programme of doing something in the world."

"Can you show me anything special that we can do in the world?"
the old man asked. His caution was wavering a little. "It is not
impossible I may be with you," he added.

The Ontarian, in fact, did not object in a spirit of cavil. He did
so apparently neither to doubt nor to believe, but simply to enquire,
for in life he was a business man. His father had left him large
lumber interests to preserve, and the responsibility had framed
his prudence. He took the same kind of care in examining the joints
of Haviland's scheme as he would have exacted about the pegging or
chains of a timber crib which was going to run a rapid.

" Why, here for instance," answered Haviland, " are great problems
at our threshold :—Independence, Imperial Federation, both of them
bearing on all advance in civilized organizations,—Unification of
Races—development of our vast and peculiar areas.   Education, too,
Foreign Trade, Land, the Classes—press upon our attention."

" You would have us awake to some such new sense of our situation as Germany did in Goethe's day ?"

" I pray for no long-haired enthusiasts.   We have business different from altering the names of the Latin divinities into Teutonic
gutturals."

" The country itself will see to that.   We have the fear of the
nations round about in our eyes," grimly said Chrysler; then he added :
" I have never known you as well as I wish, Haviland.   You speak
of this work as if you had some definite system of it, while all the
notions I have ever met or formed of such a thing have been partial
or vague."

Chamilly stood up and the firelight shone brightly and softly upon
his flushed cheek ; the dark portraits on the walls seemed to look out
upon him as if they lived, and the statue of Apollo to rise and associate its dignity with his.

" I *have* a system," he said.   " I almost feel like saying a commission of revelation.   The reason, sir, why I asked you here was that
you, my venerated friend, might understand my ideas and sympathize
with them, and help me."

He hesitated.

" I will ask you to read a manuscript, of which you will find the
first half in your room.   The remainder is not written yet."

Pierre, the butler, brought in coffee and they talked more quietly
of other subjects.

CHAPTER IV.

THE MANUSCRIPT.

"When yellow-locked and crystal-eyed,
I dreamed green woods among
*   *   *   *   *   *   *
O, then the earth was young."
—ISABELLA VALANCRY CRAWFORD.

When Chrysler went up to his bedchamber he found the following on a table between two candles :—

"BOOK OF ENTHUSIASMS.

Narrative of Chamilly d'Argentenaye Haviland.

At the Friars' School at Dormillière, racing with gleeful playmates around the shady playground, or glibly reciting frequent " Paters " and " Ave Marias," other ideas of life scarce ever entered my head ; till one day my father spoke, out of his calm silence, to my grandmother ; and with the last of his two or three sentences, " I don't destine him for a Thibetan prayer-mill," (she had fondly intended me for the priesthood) he sat down to a letter, the result of which was that I found myself in a week at the Royal Grammar School at Montreal. Here, where the great city appeared a wilderness of palaces and the large School an almost universe of youthful Crichtons whose superiorities seemed to me the greater because I knew little of their English tongue, the contrasts with my rural Dormillière were so striking and continual that I was set thinking by almost every occurrence.

A French boy is nothing if not imaginative. The time seemed to me a momentous epoch big with the question : " What path shall I follow ? "

I admired the prize boys who were so clever and famous. I took a prize myself, and felt heaven in the clapping.

I admired those equally who were skilled at athletics. I saw a tournament of sports and envied the sparkling cups and medals.

These,—to be a brilliant man of learning *and an athlete*—seemed to me the two great careers of existence !

The first step, out of a number that were to come, towards a great discovery, was thus unconsciously by me taken. What is greater than Life ? what discovery is more momentous than of its profound meaning ? Anything I am or may do is the outcome of this one discovery I later made, which seems to me the very Secret of the World.

*   *   *   *

But hold :—there is a memory in my earlier recollection, more fixed than the trees—they were poplars—of the Friars' School playground. I leaped into a seat beside my father in the carriage one day, and we drove back far into the country. Green and pleasant all the landscape we passed. Or did it pass us, I was thinking in my weird little mind ? We arrived at length at wide gates and drove up an avenue, lined by stately trees and running between broad grain fields, which led to a court shaded with leafy giants of elms and cobbled in an antique fashion; and under the woof of boughs and leaves overhead ran a very long old country-house, cottage-built. Surpassingly peaceful, and secluded was its air. It had oblique-angle-faced, shingled gables, and many windows with thin-ribbed blinds ; and a high bit of gallery. On one hand near it, under the hugest of the trees was a cool, white, well-house of stone, like a little tower. I remember vividly the red-stained door of that. On the other hand, a short distance off, commenced the capacious pile of the barns. Close at the back of the house ran a long wooded hill.

It was the ancient Manoir of Esneval—the Maison Blanche.—one of the relics of a feudal time. As we drove in and our wheels stopped, a little exquisite girl stood on the gallery, looking. Her child's face eyed us with wonder but courage for a few moments; then she ran within and, to the pang and regret of my heart, she appeared no more.

The little, brave face of the Manoir d'Esneval haunted me, child as I was, for years.

CHAPTER V.

CONFRERIE.

McGill University sits among her grounds upon the beginning of the slope of Mount Royal which lifts its foliage-foaming crest above it like an immense surge just about to break and bury the grey halls, the verdant Campus and the lovely secluded corner of brookside park. It owes its foundation to a public-spirited gentleman merchant of other days, the Honorable James McGill, whose portrait, in queue and ruffles, is brought forth in state at Founder's Festival, and who in the days of the Honorable Hudson's Bay Co.'s prime, stored his merchandize in the stout old blue warehouses* by the Place Jacques-Cartier, and thought out his far-sighted gifts to the country in the retirement of this pretty manor by the Mountain.

To that little corner of brookside park it was often my custom to withdraw in the evenings. The trees, little and great, were my companions, and the sky looked down like a friend, between their leaves. One night, at summer's close, when the dark blue of the sky was unusually deep and luminous, and the moon only a tender crescent of light, I lay on the grass in the darkness, under my favorite tree, an oak, among whose boughs the almost imperceptible moonbeams rioted. I was hidden by the shadows of a little grove just in front of me. The path passed between, about a couple of yards away.

---

* NOTE—Now turned into the restaurant called the "Chateau de Ramezay," and soon probably to be demolished.

Every stroller seemed to have gone, and I had, I thought, the peace of the surroundings to myself.

All were not yet gone, however, it seemed. The peculiar echo of steps on the hard sandy path indicated someone approaching. A shadow of a form just appeared in the darkness along the path, and turning off, disappeared for a moment into the dark grove. A deep sigh of despair surprised me. I lay still, and in a moment the form came partly between me and a glimmering of the moonlight between the branches. It was apparently a man, at least. I strained my attention and kept perfectly still. There was something extraordinary about the movements of the shadow.

Suddenly, it stepped forward a stride, I saw an arm go up to the head, both these became exposed in a open space of moonlight, and a glimmer reached me from something in the hand. Like a flash it came across me that I was in the presence of the extraordinary act of suicide. The glimmer was from the barrel and mountings of a revolver ! Those glintings were unmistakable.

I would have leaped up and sprung into the midst of the scene at once had not something else been plain at the same moment, which startled me and froze my blood.

The arm, the face, were those of my classmate Quinet ! An involuntary start of mine rustled a fallen dry branch, and the snap of a dry twig of it seemed to dissolve his determination; the hand dropped, he sprang off—and rushed quickly away in the darkness.

Quinet,—the life of this strange fellow always was extraordinary. There were several of our French-Canadians in college and they differed in some general respects from the English, but this striking-colored compatriot of mine, with his dark-red-brown hair, and dark-red-brown eyes set in his yellow complexion, was even from them a separated figure. He was fearfully clever : thought himself neglected : brooded upon it. His strange face and strange writings sometimes

published, had often fastened themselves upon me.   Now it was un-
doubtedly my duty to save him.

I followed him to his home, went up to his room and confronted
him with the whole story,—myself more agitated than he was.   I
remember his passionate state :—" Haviland, do not wonder at me.
Mankind are the key to the universe ; and I am sick of a world of
turkey-cocks.   To speak frankly is to be proscribed ; to be kind to
the unfortunate is to lose standing ; to think deeply brings the
reputation of a fool.   No one understands me.   They do not understand me, the imbeciles !—*Coglioni !*" cried he fiercely, grinding the
Corsican cry in his teeth and rising to walk about.   " As Napoleon
the Great despised them so do I, Quinet.   They never but made one
wretched who had genius in him.   And *I* have it, and dare to say that
in their faces.   The weapon for neglect is contempt !   If the
wretched shallow world can make me miserable, they can never at
least take away the delight of my superiority.   I, who would have
sympathized with and helped them and given my talents for them, shall
look down with but scorn.   Yes, I delight in these proud expressions,
I am not ashamed of testifying, and one day I shall assert myself and
make them bow to me, and shall hate them, and persecute them, and
anatomize them for the derision of each other ! "

His conduct might have seemed completely lunatical to an Englishman.   It was strange in any case.   But to me it was his physique
that was wrong, and I should see that all was put right.   " Stick to
me, Quinet," said I to him as soothingly as possible, " and I will
always stick to you.   Soyons' amis, bon marin, ' Be we friends, good
sailor ; ' and sail over every sea fearlessly.   Neither of us is understood, perhaps because our critics do not understand themselves."

" Be it so," he said, dejectedly resigning himself.

His odd colour and eyes gave a kind of unearthly tone to the interview.

I met him a few days later in almost as great a depression again.

"It's these English. I hate them. It is necessary that I should kill one."

"My dearest misanthrope," I replied, "what you need is some horse-riding."

CHAPTER VI.

ALEXANDRA.

" Maintenant que la belle saison étale les splendeurs de sa robe.
—BENJ. SULTE.

Listen ! A note is struck which, with an old magic, transforms the world ! In the dying beauty of an autumntide, Love Divine, last and most potent of the goddesses, came walking through the woods and diffused the mystery of heaven over the forest paths, the trees, the streets of the town ; and she melted intó a sweet and noble human face—a face I caught but for a moment clearly on one of our galloping rides, Quinet's and mine ; yet it remained and still looks upon me in the holy of holies of my heart's inner chapel.

"What a rare autumn ! What perfect foliage ! What cool weather ! " Quinet had wakened up beyond my expectations, and soon we were racing along, laughing and shouting repartees at each other. We reined in at last to a walk.

" Mehercle, be Charon propitious to thee when thy soul meets him at the river in Hades," he cried. " Be he propitious to thee, Chamilly, for making me a horseman ! "

Then the memorable picture ;—we speeding along that bit of road in the Park, the Mountain-side towering precipitously above us on the left and sloping below us in groves on the right ; our horses galloping faster and faster ; our dash into a bold rocky cutting ; our consternation !—a young maiden picking up autumn leaves within two yards before our galloping horses ! Near by, I remember quite clearly now her companion, and not far off the carriage with golden-bay horses.

"Stop!" I shouted.

Even as I shouted, I was already past her, and the brush of Quinet's horse flying as near on the other side of her, snatched off her bouquet of autumn leaves and strewed them in a cloud. Thank God only that we had not gone over her! The peril was frightful. My horse had had his head down and I could not pull him up.

But what excited me most was the courage of the girl. She started; but rose straight and firm, facing us as we charged. Even in that instant, I could see changes of pallor and color leap across her brow and cheek—could see them as if with supernatural vividness. Yet her eyes lighted proudly, her form held itself erect, and her clear features triumphed with the lines as if of a superior race. She could only be compared, standing there, to an angel guarding Paradise! How fair she was! And the face was the face of the little girl of the Manoir of Esneval!

After the agitations of our apologies I retained just enough of my wits about me to enquire her name. "Alexandra Grant," she said gracefully enough. Ah yes, I recollected—the Grants, within a generation, had bought the Esneval Seigniory, and its Manor-house.

CHAPTER VII.

QUINET.

Now a little more of Quinet.   Small, gaunt and strange-looking, I
pitied him because he was a victim of our stupid educational wrecking
systems.   His was too fine an organization to have been exposed to
the blunders of the scholastic managers ; for his course had exhibited
signs of no less than the genius he had claimed.   Most of his years
of study had been spent as a precocious youth in that great Seminary
of the Sulpician Fathers, the *Collége de Montréal.*   The close system
of the seminaries, however, being meant for developing priests, is
apt to produce two opposite poles of young men—the Ultramontane
and the Red Radical.   Of the bravest and keenest of the latter
Quinet was.   If newspapers were forbidden to be brought into the
College : he had a regular supply of the most liberal.   If all books
but those first submitted to approval were *tabu :*   Quinet was thrice
caught reading Voltaire.   If criticism of any of the doctrines of
Catholic piety was a sin to be expiated hardly even by months of
penance : there was nothing sacred to his inquiries, from the authority
of the Popes of Avignon to the stigma miracle of the Seraphic St.
Francis.   He was an *enfant terrible ;* Revolutionist Rousseau had
infected him ; Victor Hugo the Excommunicate was his literary idol ;
hidden and forbidden sweets made their way by subterranean passages
to his appetite ; he was the leader of a group who might some day
give trouble to the Reverend gentlemen who managed the "nation
Canadienne."   And yet, " What a declaimer of Cicero and Bossuet !

I love him," exclaimed the professor of Rhetoric, in the black-robed consultations. "His meridians do me credit!" cried the astronomical Father.

No—he was far too promising a youth to estrange by the expulsion without ceremony which any vulgar transgressor would have got for the little finger of his offences. The record ended at length with the student himself, towards the approach of his graduation, when an article appeared in that unpardonable sheet *La Lanterne du Progrès*, acutely describing and discussing the defects of the system of Seminary education, making a flippant allusion to a circular of His Grace the Archbishop, who prided himself on his style; and signed openly with the boy's name at the bottom!

Imagine the severe faces of the outraged gowned, the avoidance aghast by terrified playmates—the council with closed doors, his disappearance into the mysterious Office to confront the Directeur alone, and the interview with him at white-heat strain beginning mildly: "My son" and ending with icy distinctness: "Then, sir, Go!"

He did go. He came to the Grammar School during my last session there, and at the end of it swept away the whole of the prizes, with the Dux Medal of the school, notwithstanding his imperfect knowledge of English, and was head in every subject, *except good conduct and punctuality.*

At this he nearly killed himself. Proceeding, he carried off the highest scholarship among the Matriculants at the University, where his classical papers were said to be perfect. All through these two years and a half of College progress since, he had been astonishing us with similar terrible application and results. Professors encouraged, friends applauded, we wondered at and admired him. We did not envy him, however, for he became, as I commenced by saying, a pitiable wreck. Look at him as he stoops upon the horse!

*   *   *   *

Good old Father St. Esprit—oldest and humblest of the Order in the College—who was his friend, and whom everybody, and especially Quinet, venerated, took a private word with him before he departed from that institution.

"My son," said he, " I see the quality of thy mind, and that the Church of God will not be able to contain thee. Thou mayst wander, poor child ; yet carry thou at least in thy heart ever love of what thou seest to be good, and respect for what is venerated by another. Put this word away in thy soul in memory of thy friend the Père St. Esprit."

CHAPTER VIII.

THE TOBOGGAN SLIDE.

"What is there in this blossom-hour should knit
An omen in with every simple word?"
—ISABELLA VALANCEY CRAWFORD.

During the next few days I could do nothing of interest to me but make prudent enquiries about Alexandra Grant. I remember an answer of Little Steele's " Ah—*That* is a beautiful girl !"

" You *were* beautiful, Alexandra ! "

I caught glimpses of her on the street and in her carriage ; memory marks the spots by a glow of light; they are my holy places. I saw her open her purse for a blind man begging on a church step. I watched her turn and speak politely to a ragged newsgirl. One day, when Quinet and I, coming down from College and seeing a little boy fall on the path, threw away our books and set him on his feet, it was *her* face of approval that beamed out of a carriage window on the opposite side of the street.

I was introduced to her at the Mackenzie's, at a toboggan party given for Lockhart, the son, my friend.

Shall I ever forget our slide on the toboggan hill and my emotions in that simple question, " Will you slide with me ? "

I was already far into a *grande passion*,—foolish and desperate.

She assented, stepped over to my toboggan kindly, sat down and placed her feet under its curled front. The crown of the hill about us was illumined by a circle of Chinese lanterns, and the moon, rising in the East, reflected a dim light on the fields of snow. I lifted the toboggan, gave the little run and leaped on at the end of the cushion, with my foot out behind to steer. Immediately we shot down the first descent, and as I straightened the course of the quick-flying leaf of maple wood, I felt it correspond as if intelligently. The second descent spurred our rate to an electric speed. As I bent forward, the snow flying against my face, the sound of sliding growing louder and shriller, and my foot demanding a sterner pressure to steer, a surge of exhilarating emotions suddenly rushed over me, and a thought cried " This is Alexandra ! Alexandra whom you love."

"Alexandra !" my heart returned, " I am so near you ! " Her two thick golden plaits of hair fell just before my eyes. She was sitting calm and straight. The toboggan shot on like a flash, and the drift beat fiercely in my eyes. But why should I heed ? Away ! Away ! Leave everything behind us and speed thou out with me, love, into some region where I can reveal to thee alone this earnest soul which thou has awakened into such devotion !

Yet lo, our race slackening, the moment was even then over, and having carried us straight as an arrow, the toboggan undulated grace-fully like a serpent over a little rising in the path and came to a stand. She rose. The light of the rising moon just enabled me to still catch the threaded yellow of her hair and the translucent complexion.

One had been following us closely. " Permit me—this next is ours, Miss Grant," he said, hastening eagerly forward to her, and I saw it was Quinet.

I marked the deference which every one, old and young, paid to her, and at the house afterwards I looked on while a boisterous knot were teaching her euchre.

"Change your ace," whispered Annie Lockhart, that pretty gambler.

" But," she replied aloud in her frank, innocent manner, "*Wouldn't that be wrong ?*"

The words came to me with the force of an oracle.

" Let me bow my head," I thought. " My patron! My angel!" and as I looked upon her, passionate reverence overpowered me.

" What am I that I dare to love you and raise my eyes towards your pure light? I am not worthy to love you!"

" And you are so beautiful!"

As my meditations were pouring along in this absorbed way, a friend of ours, Grace Carter, a girl of the light, subtly graceful English type and a gay confidence of leadership, came across the room.

" O Mr. Haviland," she cried, " I've been watching your dolorous expression till I determined to learn how you do it!"

I half smiled at her, helplessly.

" It is thoroughly fifth-act. The young man looks that way when he marches around in the limelight moonlight contemplating the approach of the catastrophe. But what have you to do with catastrophes? Off the stage men only have that desperate look when they are in love. I trust you are safe, Mr. Haviland."

She looked so arch that I could not help a laugh, though the effect jarred on my mood.

" You will find me dull, I am afraid," I answered.

" That's of no consequence. Self-education is my mission. Believe me, I thirst for this knack of lugubriousness."

I would have resented the trifling at that moment from almost any person but Grace. She divined my discomfort, veered her questioning to College affairs, and detailed to me some amusing information on dances and engagements, to which I listened with what attention I could. But my eyes persisted in resting oftener and oftener on Alexandra, and some bread baked by her and Annie,—a triumph of amateur housekeeping—being passed by the latter in pieces among the cake, I imagined that it tasted like the sacrament, and utterly lost track of what the merry girl was saying. She left me to flood out her spirits on a friend who was rising to go ; whereupon I recollected myself.

Behold Quinet, poor fellow, Quinet is too earnest for Society. Some supercilious young creature has cut him to the quick for commencing a historical remark. Smarting under his rebuke he withdraws a step or two. A kind voice accosts him ; it is Alexandra. "Come here and speak to me, Mr. Quinet. You always talk what is worth while." "To talk of what is worth while makes enemies," he answered bitterly : "I am thinking of giving it up." "You should not do that," she said. "If I were a man I would think of nothing but the highest things."

The night's sleep was broken by visions of her, as I had just seen her, so near, so fair. I tried to force my imagination into snatches of remembrance of her face as colored and clear-outlined as the reality —bearing the noble expression it had worn when she said "Would not that be wrong ?"

How I sank into self-contempt by comparison !

I wonder if Englishmen feel the passion of love as we French do.

"I love her, I love her," was my burning ejaculation. "Yet how dare I love her ! I am unworthy to stand in her presence ! There is only left for me to purify and burn and subdue my heart until it is completely worthy of her holy sight. Worthy of her ! And what is worthy of her ?"

Again her presence passed before me and a voice seemed to cry "The highest things ! "

Thenceforth "The highest things" should be my search, and nothing less. My ambitions had advanced a second step.

CHAPTER IX.

ASSORTED ENTHUSIASMS.

" Ici-bas tous les lilas meurent ;
  Tous les chants des oiseaux sont courts :
Je cherche aux étés qui demeurent
      Toujours."
                                        —SULLY-PRUDHOMME.

And now of the influences which shaped that quest of " the highest things." There were the conversations in our Secret Society, the " Centre-Seekers." Picture a winter's eve, a cosy fire, a weird hall, and a group whose initiation oath was simply "I promise to be sincere."

" There is the solution of Epicurus," remarks Holyoake, our Agnostic ; " Pleasure, at least, is real. Wrap yourself in it, for you can do no better. Contentment is but one pleasure, as Salvation is another, and even sensuality may be best to you."

" How about the man who lives for his children ? " asked young Fred. Lyle, whose ruddy face was made brighter by the fire glow.

" He has his enjoyment reflected from theirs."

" What do you think of the friend in ' Vanity Fair,' who helps his rival ? "

" One of the fools," replied Holyoake, with an air of settling the matter.

Lyle reflected.

" I can't believe it that way," he said thoughtfully.

One member was Lorne Riddle ; a big bluff chap with a promising moustache, encouraged by private tuition. " Come along there,

Haviland," he exclaimed, " a nob like you should be one of the
' boys !' " These fellows don't know what life is—but to think of a
man of muscle going back on us !

" Kick not against the prigs, Riddle !" cried Little Steele in facetious delight.

" Riddle, Riddle, thou art but a poor Philistine."

" A man of Gath," contributed another.

" The Philistine has his uses. He is the successful of Evolution,"
pronounced Holyoake.

" The future will see methods better than Evolution," answered
Brether, our great firm Scotchman.

" If so, they will be of it," retorted the Agnostic.

" Now just kindly let up on that a little." Riddle continued,
" you fellows are too confounded theoretical for me. What's the
good of going round congesting your cerebrums about problems you .
can't settle ? I say let a fellow go it while he's young—moderately
you know—and when he is old he will not regret the same. You
fellows swot, and I sit in the orchestra chairs. You read your diges-
tions to rack and ruin—or else you've got to be so mighty careful,—
while I put in a fine gourmand's dinner every day, attended with the
comforts of civilization. I dance while you are working up un-
successful essays. The world owes nothing to fellows who do that.
If you're fools enough to want to benefit the world, turn your minds
to steam engines and telegraphs, that cheapen dinners and save us
running, and I'll give you my blessing in spare moments when I've
nothing do do. I take a kind of melancholy interest in this institution, you know, but honestly upon my word, I hate your rational
style, and I wouldn't for the world go round like a walking problem
and have the fellows call me ' *Forlorne* Riddle.' The place where I
enjoy myself most,—our private theatrical club,—is called the ' In-
consistents ' on that principle. We don't care about being correct.

We know we have the prettiest girls and chummiest fellows in town, and we're all right."

" Of course if a fellow's legs are so crooked that he can't dance or appear in a play, he has got to solace himself with billiards or eating, or some of the elegant accomplishments like playing the guitar. That's my system. There's philosophy in it too, by jove ! I've done lots of philosophy by the smoke of a cigarette. It's philosophy properly tamed, in evening dress. It's philosophy made into a good Churchman and Tory ! "

" La morale de la cigarette ! " suggested Quinet.

After all was not the highest thing simply to live the natural life of the time and place ?

" I refuse that," I cried to myself, " I ask a Permanent, an Eternal !."

*   *   *   *

In speculative Philosophy I sought it, urged by the saying reported of Confucius :

" The Master said : ' I seek an all-pervading Unity,' " and much useless labor did I spend upon the profound work of the monarch of modern thinkers—Immanuel Kant.

In a depression at the end of this labor I finally threw my books aside.

It was afternoon, dull and dusty: a thunderstorm was brewing. I walked to the Square. What is that carriage with golden-bay horses ? —that fresh image of loveliness—so calm—serene in queenly peace— the spiritual eyes ! " Alexandra, I am miserable ; elevate and purify my hopes with a smile, when I need thy presence—ma belle Anglaise"—No, she looks coldly and drives on in her equipage without even a recognition.—Is anything wrong ?—I am deeply dispirited. —Another street—she passes again without bowing—not even looking this time.

Wretched Haviland !—Where is mercy and what is left for me in the world ?—I will rebel about this.—I will give up trying to seek the best, and turn away from Alexandra.

At dinner that night, my grandmother said "You must go to Picault's ball, my dear ; " and my grave, oracular father added : " Yes, you shall go among our people now. I am about to send you to France."

The prospect of that journey, to which it had been my joy at other times to look forward, affected me little in my disturbed condition.

CHAPTER X.

THE ENTHUSIASM OF SOCIAL PLEASURE.

Grace Carter came over on the way to the ball, and when I descended I found her entertaining my grandmother, while a young man named Chinic, beaming with good nature and compliments, sat near her and rising with the rest grasped me by the hand as I entered. Grace too, smiling, held out her hand. As we went to the door my grandmother delivered me over to her, saying playfully : " Chamilly will be in your charge this evening. He is melancholy. C'est à toi de le guérir."

" I will be his sister of Charity ! " she cried merrily and pressed my arm. I laughed. It was not so undelightful to be taken into the companionship of a graceful girl.

As we whirled along in the carriage, the half-moon in the dark blue sky, making heavy shadows on the trees and mansions, lit her cheek and Greek-knotted hair on the side next me with a glamour so that her head and shoulders shone softly in it like a bust of Venus.

Picault's was an extensive family mansion of sandstone, built thirty years before for one of the wealthiest merchants of Montreal. It was on a corner.

One end rose into a rococo tower, lit then with the curious kind of clearness produced by a half-moon's light. In the centre, before the hospital door, projected a pillared portico, under which our carriage drove, and at the other end lurked the shades of a massive gate-way with cobbled road leading through. The carriage-road past the front was bordered by lilacs in bloom—on the one side, as we went through, all shadows, on the other faintly colored, mingling their fragrance with that of huge rose-bushes.

The doors were thrown open, and we saw a great staircase in a wide hall hung with colored lights, and entering passed into one of the most lavish of interiors. As I looked around the dressing-room to which Chinic and myself were shown and saw the windows stacked with tropical plants, the colored candles set about the walls in silver sconces; the bijou paintings and the graceful carving of the furniture; the deep blending of tints and shades in the carpets, curtains and ornaments, I felt another new experience—the sensation of luxury—and dropping back in an easy chair, asked my companion:

" Chinic, what does Picault do ? "

" Ma foi, I do not pretend to say," replied the young Frenchman, half turning towards me from the mirror where he was brushing his hair. " Suffice it he is a millionaire, and I get summoned to drink his wine. Some say he is in politics, others that he deals with stocks; for me it is enough that he deals with the dance and good table. Is it not magnificent to so live ? I would sell my soul for fifteen years of it."

The remark set me thinking a moment, but it only complicated the charm of delivering oneself over to sensations.

We met Grace at the head of the stair-case. She had never looked more Venus-like than in this fairy glow, with a plant-filled window behind her, opening out into the summer darkness. The music of a waltz of Strauss was rising from below, and I felt a wonderful thrill as she again took my arm.

Our respects being paid to the hostess, Madame Picault, Grace gave me a couple of dances on her card, and introducing me to a slender young girl, with pretty eyes, and two very long, crisp plaits of hair, went off on the arm of some one else.

As my father's plan of education had taken me hitherto wholly into English society, so far as into any, the unique feeling of being a stranger to my own race came with full force upon me for a moment and I stood silent beside the pretty eyes and looked at the scene. The walls were a perfect gallery of sublime landscapes, and small pictures heavily set; four royal chandeliers threw illumination over a maze of flowered trains and flushed complexions, moving through a stately " Lancers," under a ceiling of dark paintings, divided as if framed, by heavy gilded mouldings, like the ceiling of a Venetian Palace.

" Is it not gay—that scene there ! " I exclaimed.

" It is charming, Monsieur," said the pretty eyes. " Montreal is altogether charming."

" Ah, you come from Quebec, Mademoiselle ? "

" No, Monsieur, from New Orleans," she replied confidingly.

Now the Louisiana French are very interesting to us French of Canada. Once we formed parts of one continuous Empire, though now divided by many thousands of miles, and their fate is naturally a bond of strong sympathy to us.

" We have there only the Carnival," she continued with the winning prettiness of a child. " That is in the spring, and the young men dress up for three or four days and throw bon-bons and flowers at us. When the carnival is over, they present the young ladies with the jewels they have worn ? "

" And the ladies return them smiles more prized than jewels ? "

She looked up at me in fresh-natured delight.

" Monsieur, you must come to New Orleans sometime, during the season of the Carnival."

" I shall most certainly if you will assure me the ladies of New Orleans are all of one kind."

" You are pleased to jest, sir. But judge from my sister. Is she
not handsome ? "

Her sister,—a Southern beauty, the sensation just then of Montreal,
—was truly a noble type. The pretty one watched my rising admiration.

" What do you think of her ? "

" She is wonderful.—And she is your sister ? "

" My married sister, Monsieur. She is on her way to France. I
will tell you a little romance about her. Last year she came to Montreal
with our father, and they were delighted with it. She used to say
she would not marry a Frenchman ; nor a blonde. Above all she
detested Paris, and declared she would never live there. While she
was here she left her portrait with Mde. De Rheims as a souvenir.
Soon a young officer in the army of France comes out and visits Mde.
De Rheims and sees the picture of my sister. He was struck with it,
declared he would see the original, travelled straight to New Orleans,
and has married my sister. See him there—*he is a blonde* and *he is
taking her to Paris.*"

." How strange that is ! Montreal is a dangerous place for the ladies
of your family."

She glanced at me with sly pleasure.

" But we are not dangerous to Montreal, sir."

" Ah non, ma'm'selle."

Then this was my first type to begin on, of our French society
world. Were they all like her ? I watched the ladies and gentlemen who stood and sat chatting about, and saw that everyone else
too made an art of charming. Grace also. She frequently passed,
and I could catch her silvery French sentences and cheerful laugh.

As a partner now took away my little Southern friend, I caught
Chinic on the wing, got introduced once more, and found myself
careering in a galop down the room with a large-looking girl—Mlle.

Sylphe—whose activity was out of proportion to her figure, though in more harmony with her name. Her build was commanding, she was of dark complexion and hair, in manner demure, alluring with great power by the instrumentality of lustrous eyes, though secretly, I felt, like the tigress itself in cruelty to her victims. She was a magnificent figure, and gave me a merry dance. After it, she set about explaining the meaning of her garland decorations and the language of flowers, the Convent school at Sault-au-Recollet, dinner parties, and the young men of her acquaintance.

"You seem very fond of society?" I advanced.

"I adore society—it is my dream. I waltz, you see. I know it is wrong, and the church forbids it; but—I do not dance in Lent. After all," shrugging her shoulders, "we can confess, you know, and when we are old it will suffice to repent and be devout. I shall begin to be excessively devout," (toying with a jet cross on her necklace)—"the day I find my first grey hair."

"You have then a number of years to waltz."

Her dark eyes looked over my face as a possible conquest.

"I tremble when I think it is not for ever. But look at my aunt's and that of Madame de Rheims!"

These ladies were indeed distinguished by their hair; but I suspect that it was not the mere fact of its greyness to which she wished to draw my attention—rather it was to the manner in which they wore it, brushed up high and away from their foreheads, like dowagers of yore. Standing in a corner together very much each other's counterpart, both a trifle too dignified, they were obviously proud leaders of society. She watched my shades of expression, and cried :

"There is my favorite quadrille—Là là-là-là-là-là-à-là," softly humming and nodding her head, an action not common among the English.

"Pardon me, sir, your name is Mr. 'Aviland, I believe," interrupted a young man with a close-cut, very thick, very black beard, and the waxed ends of his moustache fiercely turned up.

I bowed.

"Our Sovereign Lady De Rheims requests the pleasure of your conversation."

On turning to Mlle. Sylphe to make my excuses, she smiled, saying with a regretful grimace : " Obeissez."

Mde. De Rheims stood with Mde. Fée, the aunt of Mlle. Sylphe, near the musicians, receiving and surveying her subjects,— a woman of majestic presence. Nodding dismissal to the fierce moustache, she acknowledged my deep bow with a slight but gracious inclination.

"Madame Fée, permit me to introduce Monsieur Chamilly Haviland, a D'Argentenaye of Dormillière,—and the last. My child, your attractions have been too exclusively of the 'West End.' You have lived among the English ; enter now into *my* society." Mde. Fée smiled, and Mde. de Rheims taking a look at me continued : "The stock is incomparable out of France. Remember, my child, that your ancestors were grande noblesse," haughtily raising her head. A novel feeling of distinction was added to my swelling current of new pleasures.

A ruddy, simply-dressed, black-haired lady, but of natural and cultured manner, was now received by her with much cordiality, and I had an opportunity to survey the whole concourse and continue my observations. Brought up as I had been for the last few years, I found my own people markedly foreign,—not so much in any obtrusive respect as in that general atmosphere to which we often apply the term.

In the first place there was the language—not patois as of *habitants* and barbers, nor the mode of the occasional caller at our house, whose pronunciation seemed an individual exception ; but an entire assemblage holding intercourse in dainty Parisian, exquisite as the famous

dialect of the Brahmans.   There was the graceful compliment, the
antithetic description, the witty repartee.   One could say the poetical
or sententious without being insulted by a stare.   Some of the ladies
were beautiful, some were not, but they had for the most part a quite
ideal degree of grace and many of them a kind of dignity not too often
elsewhere found.   Every person laughed and was happy through the
homely cotillion that was proceeding.   The feelings of the young
seemed to issue and mingle in sympathy, with a freedom naturally
delightful to my peculiar nature, and the triumphant strains of music
excited my pulses.

Mde. De Rheims touched my arm and pointed individuals by name.
" That strong young man is a d'Irumberry—the pale one, a Le Ber—
that young girl's mother is a Guay de Boisbriant.   Do not look at her
partner, he is some *canaille.*

There was, true enough, some difference.   The descendants of
gentry were on the average marked with at least physical endowments
quite distinctly above the rest of the race.   But there was a ridiculous
side, for I recognized some about whom my grandmother was used
to make merry, such as the youth who could "trace his ancestry five
ways to Charles the Fat," and the stout-built brothers in whose family
there was a rule "never to strike a man twice to knock him down."
My grandmother said that "those who could *not* knock him down
kept the tradition by not striking him once ! "

Mde. De Rheims now introduced me to two people simultaneously
—Sir Georges Mondelet, Chief-Justice, and the ruddy lady, Mde.
Fauteux of Quebec.   The Chief Justice was of that good old type, at
sight of which the word gentil-homme springs naturally to one's lips
He was small in figure, but his features were clearly cut, and the falling of the cheeks and deepening of lines produced by approach of age,
had but imparted to them an increased repose.   His clear gaze and
fine balance of expression denoted that remarkable common sense and

personal honor for which I divined his judgments and conduct must be respected. His smile was charming, and displayed a set of well-preserved teeth. The few words he spoke to me were not remarkable. They were simple and kind like his movements.

To Mde. Fauteux I offered my arm, and conducted her into the large conservatory opening off the parlors, where we walked.

"Is it not a great privilege, Monsieur, to be an Englishman?" she began with polite banter. "You are the conquerors, the millionaires; yours are the palaces, and the high and honorable places! But you, Monsieur, you are not too proud to patronize our little receptions."

"Pardon me, Madame, I am not English."

"Is that true? But you have the air."

"There is no air I could prefer to that of a man like Sir Georges Mondelet."

"Nor I too, in seriousness. That is the true French gentleman. He cares little even for his title, and prefers to be called *Mr.* Mondelet, holding his judicial office in greater esteem. I once heard him say in joke, 'that there could be many Knights but only one Chief Justice.'"

"That is true," I said.

"Yes, it is true," she echoed. "Law is a noble philosophy, and its profession the most brilliant of the highways to fame."

"Do you know," she continued, "that we inherit our law from the Romans. This beautiful system, this philosophic justice of our Province, is the imperial legacy bequeathed us by that Empire in which we once took our share as rulers of the world—the shadow of the mighty wings under which our ancestors reposed. We all have Roman blood in our veins. Do you see that face there?—that is a Roman face. Our Church speaks Latin, and looks to the city of Cæsar. Our own speech is a Latin tongue. The classics of our young men's study are still those that were current on the Forum. Our law is Roman law." *

If the gaiety of the French world had satisfied me, what was not my wonder and joy at discovering in it a reflective side ; and for half an hour I remained in a leafy alcove listening to her refined converse, —dealing with books like "Corinne," and "La Chaumière Indienne," —La Fontaine, Molière, Montesquieu,—and especially interesting me in the society which moved around us, which as she touched it with her wand of history and eloquence, acquired an inconceivable interest for me, and I was for the first time proud of being a French-Canadian.

In the midst of these excitements, as I stood so listening, and now joined by two others,—

"Chamilly, my brother, I have come for you," suddenly broke in Grace ; and stood before me all radiance, dropping somebody's arm. Excusing myself, I took her in charge and we moved gaily off. Waltzing with her was so easy that it made me feel my own motion graceful ; the swirl of mingled feelings impelled me to recognize how superior she was in other things, and to proudly set her off against each lovely or dignified or sprightly figure there ; and when the music closed abruptly, we started laughing together for the conservatory of which I have spoken, at the end of the vast rooms. This conservatory ended in a circular enlargement divided into several nooks or bowers, and we wandered into one in which the moonlight came faintly on our faces through the glass and the vines.

Again the Greek head with the light upon it !

Strains of other music floated in. Every sense was enraptured.

"Let Alexandra go !" I thought. " Let me live as my people have discovered how to live."

" Mon cher, am I tending you faithfully."

" Charmingly, my sister."

D

She laughed at the way I said it, because I spoke with perfect resignation.

The thread running through all my other experiences of the evening had been admiration of Grace.   Pleased as I was with this society, I had compared her with each of the best members of it, to her advantage.   She had in her young way, the dignity of Madame de Rheims; all the gracefulness of the Southern girl with the pretty eyes; beauty as striking, though not the same as that girl's sister; the gaiety of Chinic; and now I was to find that she was apparently as cultured as Mde. Fauteux.   For she did talk seriously and brightly about books and languages and artistic subjects:

"I would abhor beyond everything a life of fashionable vanity. My desire for life is to always keep progressing."

Whilst she talked I was reflecting, and mechanically looking around at the divisions into nooks.

"Don't you think this arrangement inviting, Chamilly?   It has a history.   An engagement has taken place in each of these alcoves except one."

I looked around at them again; then asked:

"Which is the one?"

"The alcove we are in, mon frère."

I glanced at her, the moonlight still falling brokenly upon the Venus head, and could see a crimson blush sweep over her countenance and her eyelids droop.

"Grace," I said—agitatedly, "Will you give me more of your evening after the next dance you promised?"

"Take from then to the end!—three dances that I have kept for you especially; I wish they were longer.   But I am ashamed to sit here after what I have happened to say."

CHAPTER XI.

THE "CAVE."

A whirl of rapid thoughts made it some time till I could regain presence of mind, and I found my eyes following her feverishly into the weavings of another waltz, and was roused by the "Salut, Monsieur," of a quiet man who did not know me, but turned out from his remarks, to be Picault, the owner of the mansion. His observations were general and of a kind of a conciliatory tone, and seemed to be each uttered after grave deliberation. There was a prudence and respectability and an air of inoffensiveness about his manner which indicated the quiet merchant of means. He spoke of Madame De Rheims with great respect, and drew my attention to quondam Mlle. Alvarez, the New Orleans beauty, as though her presence was a marked honor to his house ; and hearing that I was not acquainted with her, he insisted on an introduction and I found myself leading her into the alcove Grace and I had left. She spoke first of New Orleans, where English, she said, was taking the place of our language, and I gathered that the latter was becoming gradually confined to a limited circle. There was a French quarter apart from the American city, though in its midst.

"The fate of your people should make you intensely French," said I.

"Monsieur has an English descent, to judge by his name. Well then, I will say something I say at home. I do not admire Frenchmen."

" But Mlle.—your patriotism ! "

" I am not very French," she said haughtily, " My father is the son of a Spanish Minister."

" But why do you disapprove of the French ? As to me, I find them excessively attractive."

" It is because I know them well," she said gaily. " My husband is the only Frenchman I would have married. Their quest is self-gratification, to which they sacrifice no matter what. I despise them." —She laughed mock-heroically,—" Take now your Englishman ! Let him love a Frenchwoman, for it is only a Frenchwoman who can return such love ! Domestic, silent, energetic,—he adores, protects, provides, and yet accomplishes ambitions. This is because he sacrifices none of such things to the Myself, who is the god of Frenchmen ! "

These words seemed of more importance to me than the beautiful speaker could have thought. I had almost committed my soul ; was it to a cup of Comus, to a fatal household of Circe ?

The lady smilingly glided away with her husband.

Then new characteristics seemed in face of race patriotism, to dawn as I looked at those passing around. I imagined each facial expression thoughtless, heartless, jaded or disgusted. I had taken the beautiful Creole's cynical words seriously, and thought I saw the search for self-gratification everywhere.

Instead of striking a balance of impressions, I passed for the time from the extreme of admiration to the extreme of criticism, and at last turned into the supper room to think. A dapper man of sanguine complexion and grey moustache and hair, a cynical gentleman-of-leisure and old-established visitor at my grandmother's, was taking wine there, and he addressed me familiarly. I began to question him about several people :

" Who is that man with the mass of locks and the queer beard ? "

"That," replied he like a showman, "is the Honorable Grand-moulin, the National Liar, Premier Minister of the Province, and First Juggler of its finances:—a profligate in public in the name of the Church—in secret in the name of Free-Thought—*beau diseur*—demagogue of the rabble and chieftain of the Cave."

"The Cave?"

He lifted his glass of ruby liquid and faced me across it. "You may not know, my simple Ali Baba, that the Government of this Province is the private property of Forty Thieves."

"What are these thieves—this Cave?—I do not understand what you mean, sir."

"Chevaliers of the highway my child," (he had just enough in him to make him free of speech), "who obtain office through the credulity of Jean Baptiste the industrious Beaver, who, like Jacques in France, bears everything. Jean Baptiste labors. It is the duty of Jean Baptiste to believe everything he is told. Monsieur of the Forty and Company must live upon something. Tsha! The Beavers were created to sweat—to load up their pack mules and be plundered. Quebec is the cave of the Forty,—and plunder is their sesame."

"But how does such a man come to be received into society?" exclaimed I, disturbed.

The answer was prompt.

"He is successful."

Reason only too obvious. It staggered me to watch the man receiving and being greeted.

Presently I asked again : "Are more of them present?" "Assuredly. Like devils they fly in swarms : like the Apostles they never travel less than two—one to preach you the relics and the other to pick the pocket in the tails of your coat. The man with the Oriental beard there looks respectable, does he not? Tell me,—does he not?"

"It is true."

" He is the honest-man-figure-head and book-keeper of the Cave. This fellow near us," (gesturing towards a scraggy-looking little man), "has got himself appointed a judge and once securely off the raft, poses as a little tyrant to young advocates, on the Kamouraska Bench."

" What does our host, Mr. Picault do ?" I said, to change the subject.

What was my surprise when he answered :

" Picault is the Arch Devil—the organizer of the Cave—the man who manipulates the Government for the profit of his accomplices. When they require money the Province calls a loan ; it is members of the Cave who negociate it, exacting a secret commission which is itself a fortune. The loan is expended," he went on, marking each step of his narration by appropriate gestures of his right forefinger, as one who is expounding a science, " on salaries to the Cave supporters, who are appointed to ingenious sinecures. Vast contracts are given at extravagant prices to persons who pay a large share to our friends. Then the works, such as railways, are sold,—if possible to Picault, or through him in the same manner. And finally, by this system no burden is left upon the Treasury except the loan to be paid. Between this and all sorts of minor applications of the principle, though they have not long begun, the end is clear ;—yet the electorate persists in being duped by these ruffians. Men cherish their prejudices," he closed oracularly. " Men cherish their prejudices with more care than their interests."

" Until he began to control the politicans." he immediately resumed, " Picault was a bankrupt financier. Now he is nominally a banker with millions. Once bribed or scandalized, your politician is broken in ; and Picault's favourite maxim is ' You can buy the Pope, and pay less for a Cardinal.' "

" I want to get out of this house ! " I cried, no longer able to retain my indignation. " Am I a thief to associate with these criminals ?"

" My young man," said he, holding me quiet by the shoulder.
" Accept the good points of Picault and drink your lemonade. The
chieftain of fools is ever a knave ; he has been tempted by the ignorance of the people."

Such feelings of contempt and determination nevertheless took
possession of me that the relish of Picault's magnificence and the
charms of his assembly soured to very repulsion.

Indignation above all with my own self took possession of me ; for
this circle was what I was to have exchanged for the world of
Alexandra.

Must I endure to be detained here till the time of my appointment
with Grace ?   I went up to her to tell her abruptly I must go—what
reason to give I knew not—and as I looked into those trustful, believing eyes and flushed face, feelings of desperate abandon for an instant
almost overcame me.   But natural resolution increased with the
antagonism, " I must leave, Grace," said I, shortly and fiercely.   I
cannot tell you the reason.   Good night."

Next morning my father sent me to France with Quinet.

CHAPTER XII.

LA MERE PATRIE.

" Et pour la France un chant sacré s'élève ;
Qu'il brille pur, le ciel de nos aïeux ! "

—F. X. Garneau.

" Chamilly ! Chamilly ! This is the soil of our forefathers ! " Quinet and I stood at last on the shores of France. We trod it with veneration, and looked around with joy. It was the sea-port of Dieppe, whose picturesque mediæval Gothic houses ranged their tall gables before us. Hence my ancestor had sailed to the wild new Canada two centuries before.—O enchanted land !

" Behold the Middle Ages ! "—cried Quinet again, looking at the Gothic houses—" of which we have heard and read."

" Is it not strange ! "—I exclaimed—" Yes, this is the old Patrie. —Is it possible to believe ourselves here ?—Stamp and see if the ground is real ! "

" There is a *blouse !*—a *paysan,* as in the pictures—he wears the cap ! he has the wooden shoes ! "

" It is our brother—the Frenchman ! "

There was more nevertheless. Celestial angels,—I too have been in heaven. I have been a French Canadian in Paris !

Dieppe was the first note of the music, the noble and quaint Cathedral of Rouen and our railway glimpses of rural Normandy were the prelude. At last our pilgrim feet were in the Beautiful City. O much we wandered in its Avenues, with throbbing delight and love towards every face, that first memorable day. This river is the

Seine ! that Palace so proud and rich, the world-renowned *Louvre.* What is you great carved front with twin towers—that pile with the light of morning melting its spires and roofs and flying buttresses as they rise into it—that world of clustered mediæval saints in stone, beautiful, pointed-arched portals and unapproached and unapproachable dignity—from which the edifices of the City seem to stand afar off and leave it alone, and which wears not the air of to-day or yesterday ?—*Nôtre Dame de Paris,* O vast monument of French art, recorder of chivalric ages, all the generations have had recourse to thine aisles and the heart of Paris beats within thee as the hearts of Quinet and this d'Argentenaye beat under the ribs of their human breasts.

Paris knew and loved us. The fountains and great trees of the Tuilleries Gardens were palatial for us ; the Champs Elysees laughed to us as we moved through their groves ; the Arch de l'Etoile had a voice to us grandly of the victories of our race ; the Bois de Boulogne was gay with happy groups and glistening equipages.

How well they do everything in Paris ! When shall the streets of Montreal be so smooth, the houses so artistically built, when shall living be reduced to such system of neatness and saving ?

Quinet betook himself much to the obscure cheese shops and cafés in the quarters of the people, and ate and chatted with such villains that I called him "The Communard." He, on the other hand, called me "Le Grand Marquis," because I made use of some relatives who were among the nobility.

Between us we missed little. On the one hand the heart of the masses affected us. Once we bought bread of a struggling baker hard by the famous abbey of St. Denis. We asked for a cup of water to drink with it,—"But Messieurs will not drink water !" he cried, and rushed in his generosity for his poor bottle of wine.—My French-Canadian countrymen, that was a trait of yours !

I remember too,—when my shoe hurt me and I limped badly one evening along the Avenue of the Bois,—the numbers of men and women who said to one another: "O, le pauvre jeune homme," Ye world-wide Pharisees, erring Paris cannot be so deeply wicked while its heart flows so much goodness !

But the enthusiasms will run away with my story. Resolutely, *revenons.*

While Quinet, the positive pole of our expedition, was ever edging our march towards his Bastille Column and his cut-throat Quartier Montmartre, I, the negative, drew it a little into more polished circles where wit and talent sparkled. The Vicomte D'Haberville, a French d'Argentenaye, took us to a reception—not too proud of us I daresay, for the gloss of his shoes and the magnificence of his cravat outshone us as the sleek skin of a race-horse does a country filly. Especially did he eye Quinet a little coldly, so that I could scarcely persuade the proud fellow to come.

To the astonishment of the Vicomte, however, Quinet was the attraction of the evening. Taine and Thiers were there, and fired by a remark from one of these his famous men, the young Radical had ventured a clever saying.

Thiers looked at him a sharp glance as he heard the accent :

" Vous êtes des Provinces, monsieur ?"

" No, sir—from New France."

" We had once,—in America—a colony of the name," replied the statesman, reflecting.

" France has it still. It is a colony of hearts ! "

Quinet awakened interest ; was inquired into and drawn out, and we were invited to a dozen of the most interesting salons of the capital.

O but those Parisians are clever ! Why is it they are so much more brilliant than we ? Perhaps because there intellect is honored.

Quickly, through these surroundings, our knowledges and tastes advanced—Quinet's verging to the path of social science—mine to an artistic sense which suddenly unfolded into life and became my chief delight. The enthusiasm for Paris gradually led me to another offer by Life of a Highest Thing. To say it shortly—the salons led to a pleasure in the artistic, the society of artists to a growing appreciation of fine works of skill, and these, to Italy and Rome.

Do you desire to rest eyes upon the noblest products of the hand of man ? Go into the Land of Romance as we did, and wander among its castled hill-tops, its ruins of Empire, its cathedrals in the skill of whose exhaustless grandeurs Divinity breathes through genius. Meditate in reverence before the famous masterpieces of antiquity— the Venus of Milo—the silent agony of the Laocoon, the Hyperion Belvedere. Learn from Canova's pure marble, and Raphael's Chambers, and from Titian, and Tintoret, and the astonishing galaxies of intellect that shine in their constellations in the sky of the true Renaissance.

Then you may say as I did, " At length, I am finding something great and best. The beautiful is the whole that mankind can directly apprehend, and as for other things hoped for, symbolism is the true outlet for his soul. Art is the union of this beauty and symbolism. No aspiration exists but can be expressed in pleasing forms."

Does man desire God, he paints—O how raptly !—a saint ; does he feel after immortality, he sculptures an ever-young Apollo. Looking to them, he has faith, as of an oracle, in their emblematic truth, and through them instructs the world.

Art seemed to me then the Highest Thing.

CHAPTER XIII.

SOMETHING MORE OF QUINET?

One evening as we sat on the Pincian Hill, in the semi-tropical garden, overlooking the domes and towers of the Imperial City, Quinet broke our silence, and surprised me by saying abruptly :

"Let us go to England."

"What for ?"

"Let us go; I wish to go."

"But what is your press about England. I thought you hated the English."

"I do not hate the English. Among whom are there more amiable friends, more beautiful women. I am seized with a wish to see that great people in their country."

"You hated them some time ago.

"In the present tense, that verb has with me the peculiarity of parsing itself negatively."

I reflected a little on this change of opinion in Quinet, and its possible causes, till he again broke out abruptly :

"Miss Carter gave me a message for you."

The recollection of my conduct at Picault's sent a pang through me.

"What is it ?" I said. The tropical plants around us brought up vividly those at the ball."

"I did not ask her,"—his voice was curious—" what it meant, but she desired me to say for her ; 'I beg you to write me why you left the ball.' "

"So you do her page-work," I returned, for I thought I could now divine the reason of his change towards the English. " Pretty work for a grown knight !   If you know her so well, you know the picturesque groves of St. Helen's Island where she lives.   Why stop at page-work?   One would think with an enchanted isle, and an enchanting maiden, the Chevalier would find his proper occupation."

Quinet changed aspect. "Do you not then admire her?" he advanced quickly, with uncontrollable feeling.

"Not admire Grace Carter !" said I, for I felt as if I had done her injustice when I last left her,—" Yet no more than a friend, Quinet." "Is that the fact?" he cried, springing up—" I thought it was she you were in love with !   I heard you were in one of Picault's alcoves together."

CHAPTER XIV.

THE ENTHUSIASM OF LEADERSHIP.

" Dans quelle terre a borderez-vous qui vous soit plus chère que celle où vous êtes né?"
—PAUL ET VIRGINIE.

When I reached home my father took me to Dormillière, "The purpose is very special," he said, so gravely that I trusted his wisdom and hastily despatching to Alexandra a brooch of Roman mosaic, which I had bought for her in Italy, I left with him.

Life had another offer now to extend to me—Dormillière, and the power thereof. As we approached the pier, and I beheld its three green terraces one over another; the grove of pines on the hill-top above the terraces; and cottages, white, red and grey, appearing among the pines;—dear home unvisited so long;—and the spires of the Church in the sky glinting the light of the setting sun, and on the shore and pier familiar faces of old men and young men changed; boys grown into stalwart fellows, and babes into boys and girls; many quiet visions of youth rose and mingled with my thoughts, and this spell began its working, as those of Society and Art had done.

"V'la Monseigneur!" called out Pierre, our coachman, on the pier, the lineaments of whose face half seemed a memory suddenly grown vivid and real.—"Mon Dieu!" he cried laughing and crying, as he looked at me closely, "It's M'sieu Chamilly! My dear' child, it was painful to have you absent so long. Why did you not come even to see us?—Please give me your hand again. But how you are loaded! Come, where is your valise? Let me do something for you, M'sieu Chamilly."

"Les v'la!"

"V'la Monseigneur!"

"V'la M'sieu Chamilly!" the shouts went up.

"It's the young Seigneur! the young Seigneur!" spread among the villagers,—they welcomed, they addressed us, the kind spirit of French Canadians took us to itself, and I was drawn to my people, as I had not been even during the conversation of the delightful Madame Fauteux. My father received them with both hands and all sorts of gay remarks, "How do you like this, Chamilly?" he laughed, with the satisfaction of an Archduke returned to his dominions.

"Are you come to fish, Monsieur?" asked Pierre, in affectionate garrulity, as he took up the reins.

"No, good Pierre, I do not know what I am coming for."

"You will troll as formerly? Our magnificent maskinongé are polite as guests for a wedding. Yesterday I took one of ninety-seven pounds!"

The good hearted fellow kept talking as we drove.

One familiar scene after another! The village street of which I knew every doorstep. Ah!—a new wayside across in front of Widow Priedieu's—and the gay mast before the Captain Martinet's —the blacksmith's dusty shop—the inn-keepers' poles holding out their oval hotel-signs—the merry little cocked house where they had that famous jollification immortalized in the song:

"Au grand bal chez Boulé."

But my friends! my friends!—to see my old friends was the great enjoyment. "Holà," deliberate Pierre; and you three Jeans—gros Jean, grand Jean and petit Jean; "Monsieur le Notaire, bon jour!" O the faces at the panes and the heads at the door!

And lo, the gardens,—the broad fields so generous of harvest—the Manoir trees in the distance!

And as of yore,—driving up the road those merrymen in the carts singing that well remembered "En roulant":

> "Le fils du roi s'en va chassant
> En roulant, ma boulë." *

And with sympathetic exhilaration, I swing into the old life again on the current of the jovial chorus:

> "En roulant, ma boulë roulant:
> En roulant, ma boulë!"

---

* "The Dauphin forth a hunting goes.
Roll, roll on, my rolling ball."
—OLD CHANSON.

CHAPTER XV.

THE LIFE OF LEADERSHIP.

......" Pourvu qu'ils vivent noblement et ne fassent aucun acte dérogeant à noblesse."
PATENTS OF NOBLESSE.

"Light the lamps," my father ordered.

Tardif, the butler, did so with alacrity.

"Tardif, thou canst withdraw," added my father.

"Oui, monseigneur," replied Tardif, bowing respectfully, and went.

The room and its antiquated splendors looked ancestral to me. Its size struck me. It was larger than any in our town house. The family portraits and furniture revived lifelong memories. We had a fine collection of forefathers.

"Chamilly"—began my father, walking up before the picture of one who was to me childhood's holy dream. He stopped for some moments, gazing up to her face with intense affection, and then turning to me, said in a broken voice—"Never forget your mother."

"No, sir," I replied, bending my head.

In a moment he went on to the other portraits, and his manner altered to more of pride.

"Your grandfather, the Honorable Chateauguay, this. This is his Lady, your grandmother. Here is her father, a LeGardeur de Repentigny. There is the old Marshal in armor. Here is Louise d'Argentenaye, of the time of Henry IV., who married a Montcalm. Here is the Count d'Argentenaye in armor." And thus he took me about on a singular round, and informed me concerning the whole gallery.

He stopped at an old, solid wood cabinet, with spiral legs, bent over and opened it with a key.

" Now," thought I, " these mysteries are going to be explained."

" This is a dress sword," he went on, "worn in France, at the court of Louis XIII. It was worn by one of your forefathers. Here are two decorations—Crosses of St. Louis—what beautiful little things they are. They belong to two of us who were Chevaliers."

I was only still more mystified.

" Come into the office, my son," said he, leading me into a room used for collecting the feudal rents and other business.

" It is coming now," I exclaimed to myself.

My father lifted out an iron box, ornamented with our arms in color, and handed to me a parchment, having an immense wax seal, which I took and read.

" Louis de Buade, Comte de Frontenac, Councillor of the King in his Councils of the State and Privy Council, Governor and Lieutenant-General of His Majesty in Canada, Acadia, and other countries of Septentrional France. " To All Those who shall see these present "letters : HIS MAJESTY having at all times sought to act with " zeal proper to the just title of Eldest Son of the Church, has " passed into this Country good number of his subjects, Officers of his " troops in the Regiment of Carignan and others, whereof the " most part desiring to attach themselves to the country by founding " Estates and Seigniories proportionate to their force ; and the Sieur " JEAN CHAMILIE D'ARGENTENAY, Lieutenant of the Company of " D'Ormillière, having prayed us to grant him some such : WE, " in consideration of the good, useful, and praiseworthy services he " has rendered to His Majesty as well in Old France as New, do " concede to the said Sieur Jean Chamilie D'Argentenay, the Extent " of Lands which shall be found on the River St. Lawrence from " those of Sieur Simon de la Lande to those heretofore granted to

"the Sieur de Bois-Hébert, to enjoy said land *en Fief et Seigneurie*
"at charge of the Faith and Homage, the said Sieur Jean Chamilie
"D'Argentenay his heirs and representatives shall be held to render
"at Our Castle of St. Louis at Quebec."

" DE FRONTENAC."

I laid down the parchment.

"This is the original grant of the seigniory ?"

" Yes," he replied with animation, "The ' HIS MAJESTY ' there
is the Grand Monarque himself ! De Frontenac is the Great
Count, and that Jean Chamilly D'Argentenaye, cadet of the Chamillys
of Rouen, is our first predecessor on these lands."

Taking a large genealogical tree out of the box, and spreading
it on the table, he showed me my descent. " The Honorable
Chateauguay drew this up at the time of my marriage," he began.

"The whole tree is mine then ?" I ventured, surveying it.

" Yes," he cried, "and these are brave and honorable names ! The
wish of my heart has been that you preserve their record. See : the
first marriage is a Mlle. Boucher de Boucherville, whose father, Pierre,
Governor of Three Rivers, was so honest and wise in the perilous
early course of the Colony ! Madeline de Verchères, heroic holder of
the fort surprised by Iroquois, is near her. See ! we date from the
fourteenth century, and are allied with the Montaignes, Grammonts,
Sullys, La Rochefoucaulds. Here is Le Moyne d'Iberville, and there
De Hertel, brave and able,—a Juchereau du Chesnay ; a Joybert
de Soulanges. Down here is De Salaberry, the Leonidas of Lower
Canada. There behold Philippe de Gaspé, who wrote ' Les Anciens
Canadiens ;' there Gaspard Joly, the Knight of Lotbinière.—But
you can inform yourself about these names. They will be useful
in your enterprises by raising you above the reproach of being an
adventurer. Seat yourself over there."

"My father," thought I to myself, "you and your pride are both very much out of date," but I obeyed him and seated myself where he indicated.

"The reason why I have brought you here, is to tell you, that it has always been intended that you should in some way, succeed in these properties. Before you developed, it was not possible to predict exactly how you might do it; but within the last few years you have surpassed our hopes; and I have no trepidation in putting before you my views of your future position. You may think I am strong in health, but I shall soon pass away."

My heart suddenly started.

"And you will find yourself here with revenues ample for the moderate purposes of a gentleman. You may live in the country, or in the city, as you please; but my desire is that you should live here, and continue in the paths of your grandfather and myself: for he was a just Englishman, and taught me that no one must take without an equivalent; and that a landlord owed duties to his people, of the value of the moneys they paid him. Formerly the lord gave his vassals armed protection for their rents: now there is nothing to which the law forces him; thus his returns must be fixed by his sense of duty."

"Do not fear that I am proposing anything too sombre, Chamilly: It is an agreeable life. There is no demand for your being shut up in the place; and one can surround himself very conveniently with his private tastes."

But I did not feel the scheme repugnant. The house and locality had struck me before as a comfortable retirement to prosecute the study of Art, "and perhaps, I might bring here"—(I dared not put her name into syllables in such a flight of hope.)

"You will find, though, more than you anticipate to do"

I looked up.

"And greater undertakings to accomplish properly than I have been strong enough to meet."

"What do you mean, sir?" I enquired.

"These poor simple people," he said, "have many enemies, and they sometimes do not know their friends. You are their hereditary guardian. Instead of mediæval protection, you must give them that of a nineteenth century Chief.

"A nineteenth century Chief?" I could not but exclaim, "What is a nineteenth century Chief?"

"The people's friend and leader."

"Yes, but what am I to do, sir?"

"In the first place, discourage litigation and its miseries. Offer mediation wherever you can. Keep drink out of the villages. Preserve the ancient forms of courtesy. Grow timber, and introduce improvements in farming."

He spoke of other things. I was to fight especially the Ultramontanes and the demagogues. My father was an uncompromising Liberal of the old school.

"But what can I do about this?" I asked, my artistic skies beginning to cloud with the prospect.

"You can speak! I know you will make an orator. You will be a member at Quebec; and then you can effect something. I mourn over the state of affairs, but I do not fear for the true end; and I yearn, as if across the grave to see the vigor of another generation of us pressing into the struggle. Remember our ancient motto," and he laid his finger on the little coat of arms on the iron box, with its scroll : "*Sans Hésiter.*"

I did not answer him, but sat thinking, while gathering up the documents into the box, he carried it back to the office.

END OF THE FIRST PART OF THE
BOOK OF ENTHUSIASMS.

When Chrysler arrived next morning at the break in Chamilly's manuscript, the sun was rising high and shining upon the river and front hedge, and on the green lawn before the Ontarian's window, and he could see Haviland walking backwards and forwards meditatively across the grass waiting for him to descend to breakfast. He hurried down, and as he came to his host, remarked, "The drift of your story is not quite clear to me."

"I wish I had the sequel written," the young man replied, "I am trying to lead on to a great matter."

BOOK II.

CHAPTER XVI.

A POLITICAL SERMON.

"In the crowded old Cathedral all the town were on their knees."
—D'Arcy McGee.

"That's not preaching *la morale*. And it's *actionable !*" a vigorous man energetically gesticulated among the crowd in the Circuit Court Room.

The subject of excitement was a sermon by the Curé.

Messire L'Archeveque, of Dormillière, was in most respects an unimpeachable priest. He ministered to the sick faithfully, after the rites of the Church, he gave to the poor, he rendered unto Cæsar. But—but, he hated Liberalism. On this point he was rabid ; and as his Reverence was a stout, apoplectic person, of delivery and opinions not accustomed to criticism, it sometimes laid him somewhat open to ridicule.

How the sermon was delivered, matters little to us. Suffice it that it was a bold denunciation of the Liberals, named by their party name, and that there were some strong expressions in it :

"My brothers—when the priest speaks, it is not he who speaks, —but God.

"My brethren, when the Priest commands you, it is the Church which commands you ; and the voice of the Church is the voice of the Eternal." .   .   .   .   Look at France. Remind yourselves what she was in the centuries of her faith, devout and glorious, the lily among the kingdoms of the earth, because she was the Eldest

Daughter of the Church. Behold her at this time, among the nations, dying in the terrible embraces of FREE-MASONRY !!

"Take warning by her, brethren. Follow her not! It is the Liberals who have done this. Crush out the seeds of that doctrine ! Let the spirits which call themselves by this name never have peace among you. Avoid them ! Distrust them ! Have nothing to do with that people ! May the wrath of our Father descend upon them, the damnation of the infernal dungeons ! and—" he brought down his book's edge loudly on the pulpit,— "the excommunication of the Church of God, Catholic, Apostolic, Roman ! "

The book was taken up once more, and slamming it down again with all its force, the good curé turned and waddled from the pulpit.

$$*\qquad*\qquad*\qquad*\qquad*$$

Since the first moments when Chrysler's eyes rested on the village of Dormillière from the steamer's deck, the observations of the place and its people were to him a piquant and suggestive study.

He had been there but a few hours when he discovered its central fact. The Central Fact of Dormillière was the Parish Church.

First, it was the centre in prominence as a feature of the view, for with the exception of the Convent school, no one of the string of cottages and buildings, stone, brick and wood, which constitute the single street of the place, presumed to rival it even in size, but all of them disposed themselves about it, and, as it were, rested humbly in its protection, particularly the Convent school itself, a plain red-brick building, which stood by its side.

It was also the centre by position ; being situate about mid-way between the ends of the long street, standing back commanding the only square, which was flanked on its two sides by the sole other edifices of public character, the priest's residence, or *presbytère*, and the friars' school for boys.

It is needless to say that the Church was the central fact

architecturally also. Large and of ancient look, its wrinkled, whited, rude-surfaced face was impressive, notwithstanding that it was relieved by but little ornament; for its design was from the hand of some bygone architect of broad and quiet ability.

Be in no hurry, friend reader, but let us look it over, for it is an antiquity, and worthy of the title.

The façade consisted of a great gable, flanked by two square towers. The gable roof had a steep mediæval pitch, and was pinnacled by the statue of a saint. A small circular window was set in the angle, and looked like the building's eye. Three larger windows and the great door came below in the broad front at their proper stages of the design; and in the centre a cut stone oval, bore the date " 1761," in quaint figures—a date that seemed a monument of the fatal storming of Quebec, just over, and the final surrender of Montreal, just to be made—the end of French dominion over three quarters of North America !

A number of details afforded entertainment to the curious eye. There were the rude capitals "St. J. B." and "St. F. X." on the keystone of the round-arched side doors at the foot of the towers. There were the series of circular windows leading one above another, on the towers, up to the charming belfry spire which crowned them. There were high up in the air on the latter, the fleur-de-lys and cock weather-vane, symbolical of France. Nine gables too, had the church, of various sizes. Its roof was shingled and black, and where it sloped down in the rear, a little third belfry pointed its spire. A stout, stone sacristy grew out behind. A low pebbled platform, two steps high, extended in front, and had a crier's pulpit upon it. And amid these varied features, the body of the church on all sides cloaked itself in its black roof with a mien of dignity, and its graceful tin-covered belfries, fair in their mediæval patterns and pointing sweetly to heaven, glinted far over the leagues of the River.

Yet it was not alone as to prominence of appearance, situation, and architectural attractiveness—that Dormillière found its centre in the Parish Church. No relation of life, no thought, no interest, no age in years, but had its most intimate relation with it. There alike weary souls crept to pray for consolation, and vain minds sought the pomp of its ecclesiastic spectacles and ceremonies; the bailiff cried his law-sales before it, the bellman his advertisements; there was holy water for the babe, holy oil for the dying, masses for the departed; the maiden and the laborer unveiled their secret lives in its confessional-box; and all felt the influence, yea some at that period, the sternly asserted rule, of the Master of the institution.

Chamilly went with Chrysler to it on the first morning of his stay in Dormillière, which was a Sunday. As they approached it through the square, filled with the tied teams of the congregation, a beadle, gorgeous in livery of black and red, with knee-breeches and cocked hat, emerged from the side door and proceeded to drive the groups of stragglers gently inwards with his staff, as a shepherd guides a flock.

Haviland looked at his friend, smiling.

"You are not in Ontario," he said.

"Clearly not," replied Chrsyler, "In my democratic Province, such a proceeding would be impossible."

When they entered, the gorgeous beadle led them soberly up one of the aisles,—carrying his staff in a stately manner—to the seigniorial pew, a large, high enclosure, with a railing about the top like a miniature balustrade, and a coat-of-arms painted on the door; and into this he ushered them with grave form, and the Ontarian vividly began to realize that he was in a feudal land: after which he took a glance about him.

Filling the great phalanx of soiled and common pews in the nave, were the first representative mass of French-Canadians whom he had been brought to face. "Here," he thought, "are those who speak the partner voice in our Confederation, and whom we should know as brothers."

A few stood out in the quality of parts of the whole, but only to emphasize it as a mass. Above the crowd, he marked, for instance, the sober, responsible faces of the Marguilliers. A girl's face too, particularly attracted him—that of one who sat beside the Sisters attendant over the convent children in their gallery. No romantic seraphicness glowed upon her features or her form ; but she was following the service with the light of simply such spiritual earnestness and intelligence about her that she seemed to sit there a superior being. But it was the faces of the laborer and the solid farmer that oftenest dotted the surface of the sea of heads. So typical to him were the features and responses of all, that he could not shake off the feeling that it was not individuals he saw, but a People.

A People ! No flippant thing is it to feel oneself in the presence of so great an Organism. If some hour of one man's pain, or of the grandeur of some other one, may be thought-worthy things, how reverently must breath be hushed as we stand in presence of a race's life, and think we hear its sorrows, cries and voices ! Ever, thou People's Song, must thou stir the heart that listens, sweeping its tenderest chords of pity, and chanting organ music to its aspirations.

The curé's sermon following as before detailed, the congregation appeared oppressed with its denunciation, but it produced no effect whatever upon Haviland, the Liberal leader, whose countenance rested its dark eyes on the tablets of his ancestors in the transept wall before him.

CHAPTER XVII.

ZOTIQUE'S RECEPTION.

A noble looking man of fifty years, stood waiting to meet them as they made their way out. Of olive complexion, small cherry mouth and features, yet fine head and person, and smiling benignly, he advanced a step before Chrysler noticed him.

"Salut, M'sieu l'Honorable," bowed Haviland.

"Good-day, Chamilly," he replied quickly, without ceasing to smile directly towards the other man and holding out his hand.

Chrysler looked closer at his features.

"Ah, Mr. Genest!" he exclaimed, with pleasure, recognizing the Hon. Aristide Genest, a personage potent in his time in Dominion Councils.

"I hope now to know the gentleman as completely as I have admired him," Genest complimented in the French way, twinkling his eyes merrily. "Many a time I have listened to your advices in the Parliament. I say to you 'Welcome.'"

Chamilly started off to talk with his innumerable constituents in the crowd.

"Let us cross over here, sir, and hear what they have to say about the sermon," proposed Genest.

They crossed to a stone building on the other side of the road, and passed through a group of countrymen into a hall of some length, where sat sunk in a rustic rocking-chair, a singular individual, whose observations seemed to be amusing the crowd.

In appearance, he reminded one of no less remarkable a person than the Devil, for he bore the traditional nose and mouth of that gentleman, and his body was lean as Casca's; but he seemed at worst a Mephistopheles from the extravagance of the delivery of his sarcasms.

The subject of discussion was the sermon.

"Baptême, it is terrible!" exclaimed the cadaverous humorist. "Ever this indigenous Pius IX—fulminating, fulminating, fulminating!—Too much inferno. The curé does half his burning for Beëlzebub! We are served in a constant auto-da-fé."

"Heh, heh, heh," creaked an old skin-and-bones, with one tooth visible, which shook as the laugh emerged. Stolid men smoking, deigned to smile.

People seemed prepared to laugh at anything he said.

"What is it that an auto-da-fé is?" a young man demanded from a corner.

"You don't know auto-da-fés?—A dish, my child.—An auto-da-fé is Liberal broiled."

The character of the room, at which Chrysler now had time to glance, explained itself by a large painting of that lion-and-unicorn-supporting-the-British-arms, which embellishes Courts of Justice. "This room is the Circuit Court," Genest remarked—"Zotique there, calls it the Circuitous Court—A very poor pun is received with hospitality here."

"I should like to know that man," said Chrysler.

"Nothing easier. Zotique, come here, my cousin."

He caught sight of them, and rising, without altogether dropping his broadly humorous expression, extended an invitation to take his rocking-chair, which Chrysler accepted.

Zotique was like the Mephistopheles he resembled, one of those who have been every where, seen much, done everything. Born respectably,—a cousin of l'Honorable's—he had executed in his younger days a record of pranks upon the neighbors, which at a safe distance of time became good humoredly traditional. The trial and despair of Père Galibert, and the disapproved of Chamilly's father, he ran away to Trois-Rivières as soon as he knew enough to do so; thence to Montreal, and Joliette; and a Fur Post near Saipasoù (or, "Nobody-knows-Where," for Zotique asserts the region has that name); then was a veracious steamboat guide for tourists to the Gulf; edited a comic weekly at Quebec, "illustrated" it, itself cheerfully and truly confessed, "with execrable wood-engravings;" as Papal Zouave, he embarked for Rome to gallant in voluminous trousers on four sous a day; fought wildly, for the fun of it, at the Pia Gate against Victor Emmanuel's red-shirted patriots, — and came back to Dormillière disgusted. The Registrarship of the county being vacant, a pious government appointed him to the position, upon recommendation by the "high Clergy," as a martyr for the good cause; and on a similar sacred ground he obtained the passage of a private bill through the Legislature, admitting him to the honorable profession of notary without the trouble of studying.

So it came to pass that our friend was installed in the Registry Office end of the long cottage known as the Circuit Court House, and made use of the Court Hall itself for his Sunday receptions to the people.

The people themselves were worth a brief catalogue.

Jacques Poulin, the horse trader, stood against a window, with his big straw hat on. His trotting sulky was outside. Gagnant, -the established merchant, with contented reticence of well-to-do-ness, was remarking of some enterprise, "It won't pay its tobacco." Toutsignant, his insecure and overdaring young rival, who was bound to cut trade, and let calculation take care of itself, sat on the opposite side of the room, and, bantering with him, the shrewd *habitants,* Bourdon and Desrochers, who were to profit by his theory of an advance in rye. The young doctor, Boucher from Boucherville, leaned near, superior in broadcloth frock coat, red tie, and silk hat. Along a bench, squeezed a jolly half-dozen *"garçons,"* and a special mist of tobacco smoke hung imminent over their heads. About the floor, the windows, the corners of the room, the bar of the court, sat, lounged, smoked, and stood, in friendly groups, a host of neighbors, amiably listening, more or less, to Zotique's harangues and conversations. It cannot be said, however, that they abated much of their own little discussions. Every now and then some private Babel would break in like a surge, over the general noise, and attract attention for an instant.

"The auto-da-fé — alas, it recalls me the ravishing country of Spain ! O those Sierras !—those Vegas ! the mountains shining with snow ! the green plains watered !—but misère ! hot as—the disposition of the Curé. To-day, gentlemen, the affair becomes serious, for lo, the approach of a doubtful election, and a trifle of clerical interference, like a seed upon the balance, might well—" the sentence was appendixed by an explosive shrug.

"Now, the Council of war ! we must have a command to him from the Bishop; and it is I, Zotique Genest, as prominent citizen ! as Registrar ! as *Zouave* ! who will write and get it.

"But more—that sacré Grandmoulin is coming, and we must receive him at point of bayonet, *á la charge de cuirasse !* that sacré Grandmoulin !"

"He will be received !" called out a voice.

"The National Liar !" proposed another.

"The breach in our wall is the Curé," continued Zotique.

"Mais."

> Qu'allons nous faire,
> Dans çette galère ? . . . .

"If we could only strap him up with every mark of respect, like the sacred white elephant of the Indies!—But first, the Bishop's order! Remark my brother, I am not advocating disobedience :—only coercion."

The laugh rose again. It was not so much anything he said, but his extraordinarily grotesque ways—a roll of his large eyes, or a drawing down of his long, thin mouth, with some quick action of the head, arms or shoulders, that amused them.

"Me, I say *sacré* to the Curés," boasted a heavy, bleared fellow, stepping forward and looking round. His appearance indicated the class of parodies on the American citizen, known vulgarly as "Yankees from Longueuil," and as he continued, "I say to them,"—he added a string of blasphemy in exaggerated Vermontese.

"Be moderate, Mr. Cuiller," Zotique interposed, "None of us have the honor of being ruffians."

"In the Unyted Staytes," continued Cuiller, however, jerking his heavy shoulder forward, "when a curé comes to them they say 'Go on, cursed rascal,'" More oaths in English. The hearers looked on without knowing how to act, some of them, without doubt, in that atmosphere, tremblingly admiring his hardihood.

"Cuiller,"—commenced the Honorable, easily.

"My name is Spoon," the Yankee from Longueuil drawled, "I've got a white man's name."

Cuiller, in fact, was of the host who have Anglicised their patronymics. Many a man who goes as "White" in New England, is really Le Blanc ; Desrochers translates himself "Stone," "Monsieur Des Trois-Maisons calls himself "Mr. Three-Houses," and it is well authenticated that a certain Magloire Phaneuf exists who triumphs in the supreme ingenuity of "My-glory Makes-nine."

"There 'is a respect due," proceeded the Honorable, ignoring the correction "to what others consider sacred, even by those who themselves respect nothing. This gentleman, besides, sir, is an English gentleman, and your use of his tongue cannot but be a barbarism to his taste."

The big fellow shoved his hands into the hip pockets of his striped trousers; and putting on a leer of pretended indifference, turned to a man named Benoit, who was regarding him with admiration.

This was an orator and a Solomon. He was a farmer, middle-aged, and somewhat short, whose shaven lips were drawn so over-soberly as to express a complete self-conviction of his own profundity, while his unstable averted glance warned that his alliances were not to be depended on where he was likely to be a material loser. A particularly "fluent" man, accomplished in gestures such as form an ingredient in all French conversation, he was in Zotique's Sunday afternoons a zestful contestant. His clothes were of homespun, dyed a raw, light blue, and he was proud of his choice of the color, for its singularity.

"Monsieur Genest," he began, with oratorical impressiveness, coming forward, and bowing to Zotique, "Monsieur l'Honorable; Monsieur;" bowing low; "and Messieurs. I speak not against the clergy, whom the good God and His Pontifical Holiness have set over us for instruction and guidance. I am not speaking against those holy men. But it seems to me to-day that you, my friend, are a little rash—a very little severe—in reproaching my friend, Mr. Cuiller, upon the language which he uses, coming from a foreign country where neither the expressions, nor the customs, are the same as ours; and it seems to me that there is a point a little subtle which should have been noticed by you before commencing, and on which I dare to base my exception to the form; and this point is, I pretend, that Mr. Cuiller has said nothing directly himself against the clergy, but has simply told how they were treated in the United States."

This beginning, delivered with appropriate gestures—now a bow, now an ultra-crossing of the arms, only to throw them apart again, now a chopping down with both hands from the elbow, now again a graceful clasping of them in front, made a satisfactory impression on Benoit himself, who prepared to continue indefinitely had not Zotique interrupted.

"Benoit, you are too fine for good millstone. But respecting friend Cuiller, we are willingly converted to your delusion. He is honorably acquitted of his crime."

"And now," he cried, "Oyez! Let all who have not forgotten how to make their marks, sign the requisition which I observe in the hands of Maître Descarries."

Maître Descarries, Notary, an elderly, active little man, carefully attired and wearing his white hair brushed back from his forehead, in a manner resembling a halo, or some silvery kind of old-time wig, stood at the door holding a document,—a paper nominating Sieur Chamilly Haviland to represent the Electoral District of Argentenaye.

The Notary, advancing, laid it on the bar of the Court, and everybody crowded to look on and see those requested to sign do so.

The Honorable, the first to be called, went forward and affixed his name, and Maître Descarries turned to a person who was apparently an old farmer, but a man with a face of conspicuous dignity.

"Will you sign, Mr. De La Lande?"

"Ah yes, Monsieur Descarries—'with both hands,'"—answered he, bowing quickly; and his signature read, to the Ontarian's astonishment: "De La Lande, Duke of St. Denis, Peer of France."

Thus, at this after-mass reception, Chrysler was introduced to a circle of whom he was to see much in the events to follow.

CHAPTER XVIII.

THE AMERICAN FRANCE.

Chrysler and Genest, after reaching the Manoir, sat conversing under the large triple tree on the side of the lawn.

"You have no idea of the simplicity of life here," l'Honorable philosophised. "We dwell as peacefully, in general, and almost as much in one spot as these great trees. After all, is there any condition in which mortal existence is happier than that of pure air and tranquility. We have a proverb, 'Love God and go thy path.' To love God, to live, to die, are the complete circle."

Chamilly's entrance put an end to these idyllic observations. He was driven up in a cart by a country jehu, and leaping out, there followed him a couple of friends.

Haviland called Tardif, the head servant, who appeared at the door of the house, bareheaded, with an apron on:

"Bring the dinner out here, Tardif," he ordered; and a light table was set under the spreading boughs.

"Now tell us, De La Lande, about your trip to Montreal."

Of the two friends who drove up with their host in the cart, one was Brebœuf, a hunchback. This little creature on being introduced, bowed and shook hands with an aspect of hopeless resignation, and sitting down, relapsed into thought, telescoping his neck into his squarish shoulders. His companion was a young man of small build, but spirited, good-looking face—De La Lande, schoolmaster of the village, a son of the farmer "Duke."

"And where commence?" responded the schoolmaster to the request for an account of the trip to Montreal.

"In the middle, as I am doing," retorted Haviland, flourishing the carving-knife over the joint.

"Ah well. The middle was the climax with me. It was the Fête of St. Jean Baptiste?"

"You saw Notre Dame, and the great procession?" inquired the Honorable.

" Yes, I saw that vast Cathedral fifteen thousand full! And the Curé of Colonization climbed up in the midst, and I heard the most glorious words that were ever spoken to French Canadians!"

" Was the procession like ours here?"

"At Dormillière? Pah!—we have two Curés, a beadle and the choir-boys! Theirs was a mile in length. There were nineteen bands playing music, all in fine uniforms, and there were all the Societies of St. Jean Baptiste walking, with their gold chains and their badges, and as many as forty magnificently decorated cars, bearing representations of the discovery of Canada by Jacques Cartier, and the workings of all the trades, and innumerable splendid banners, of white, and blue, and red and green, with gold inscriptions and pictures—and the Curé of Col—"

" Were the streets well decorated? How were the arches and flags?"

"They were good. The streets were full of flying tricolors and Union Jacks stretched across them. They were lined with green saplings as we do here. The crowd was enormous. There were thousands from the States. And the Cathedral of Notre Dame was all excitement; for the Curé—,"

" Tell us about it! Every one speaks of it! What did he say!

(A well-known priest had just electrified the people of the land with an extraordinary declaration.)

" But, to speak of his aims, I must recollect the numbers of our people."

" Brebœuf, mon brebis," said Chamilly, turning to the little fellow, "what is the number of the French Canadians ? "

The hunchback lifted his face gravely, and issued in a monotonous voice, but with the precision of a machine :—" One million, eighty-two thousand, nine hundred and forty-three, in Canada, by the census of 1870 ; one million, one hundred and ten thousand, in Canada, by the computation of the Abbé Zero; four hundred and thirty-five thousand in the United States by the computation of the same."

The Ontarian was surprised at his odd, machine-like accuracy, but Haviland only laughed a little chuckle and Chrysler's glance was drawn away towards a figure entering the gate, walking abstractedly, his hands in his hip pockets and eyes on the path. He was of slender but agile person, the decision which marked every movement showing his consciousness of latent activity. Haviland espied him presently :

" Bravo, here is Quinet. Quinet, what are you doing ? "

" Cultivating dulness," replied the figure, scarcely glancing up.

" Come and cultivate us, for a contrast, my friend."

" Would I be changing occupation ?"

" Sit here and we will show you. Yourself may be as dull as you like."

The stranger, nonchalantly, and half-defiantly, seated himself, after introduction. Chrysler scanned him curiously in recollection of the references to him in Haviland's Book of Enthusiasms, and recognized the strange red-brown scale of hues of hair, eyebrows and moustache, which gave character to his appearance ; but the pale countenance was strong now, and tanned, though spare, and all the signs of former weakness had departed.

Chamilly continued to Chrysler:

"I am not a little proud of the cheerfulness, the spirit, the respectability, the intelligence of my little people. And if you had seen the mottoes which I have read on cars and banners in the processions of our national saint; such as, "GOD HAS MADE LAW TO EVERY MAN TO LABOR," and : "TO MAKE THE PEOPLE BETTER,"—you would have felt with me that it must be a people responsive to sober and admirable aims."

"I have no doubt of it," remarked the visitor genially.

"But I scarcely think you can be familiar with a group of startling projects lately cherished in our circles."

"Plots against everybody," Quinet remarked. "Have the goodness to pass me the asparagus."

"The Continent of North America is a large acre," continued Haviland. "Can you fancy a race who a century ago were but ninety thousand, aspiring and actually planning for its complete control?"

Chrysler looked amused at the idea, for the handful of French-Canadians.

"That is our firmly-persuaded future!" asserted the young man, De La Lande, eagerly and boldly. "The Curé of Colonization has demonstrated that it is possible. We shall reconquer the continent!"

"Is it your view?" Chrysler asked of Chamilly.

"I instance it," he returned, "because it shows that my people are capable of thinking high."

"There is a progression of plans!" went on the eager De La Lande. "The first is to get control of the six English counties!"

"I will trust the Anglo-Saxon for holding his own," the Ontarian laughed, in the amusement of vigorous confidence.

"But we gain!" the young man cried. "Our race is always French! We win fast the British strongholds in our dear Province."

"This the least, of the plans," Haviland remarked. "All are founded on a curious fact."

"What fact is that?"

"Our phenomenal multiplication in numbers," returned the seigneur, smiling.

"What?" cried Chrysler.

He stopped a moment open-eyed, and then laughed heartily and long. He could not satisfy his laughter at such a basis for conquest of a continent, and it burst forth again at intervals for some time.

"Nevertheless it is true,—and Biblical," continued the undaunted schoolmaster. *"Sicut saggittae in manu potentis, ita filii excussorum."*

"Brebœuf," said Haviland, who took some part with De La Lande but joined in Chrysler's amusement, "help us. What was the number of French-Canadians at the conquest by the English?"

"Sixty-nine thousand two hundred and sixty-five, by the census of the General Murray in 1765, including approximately 500 others."

"And now?"

"One million and eight-two thousand nine hundred and forty, by the census of 1870."

"You see, sir, what a growth. The clergy encourage it with satisfaction. It is not comfortable for bachelors in some of our parishes."

All at the table were laughing, more or less, except De La Lande and the hunchback, who were perfectly serious.

"One plan, sir, I confess freely," said the former, affects yourself. You are perfectly acquainted with the Ottawa River, separating your Province from our own, and that it cuts across and above yours, which is a peninsula. The fourth great plan (out of six), is to plant centres along the Ottawa which shall exert their expansive force downwards to overrun your peninsula."

"What a dangerous race!"

"While another contingent meets it further south, where our progress is well known. So we shall win the centre itself of the Dominion. Let us possess the North, says our Peter the Hermit, and we can rest sure of the whole. Yes, let us possess the North! let us populate the shores of Hudson's Bay!" the enthusiast cried, losing himself in his vision, "Let us possess the shores of Hudson's Bay, where d'Iberville of old dislodged our enemies!"

"Peter the Hermit!" laughed Chamilly. "What a name for our jolly old Curé of Colonization. But all that is well enough for ecclesiastics to recommend, since none others would invite their friends to die on those refrigerated wastes.—Yet the people themselves are heroically willing."

"Our next ambition," proceeded De La Lande, absorbed in his enthusiasm and quite guileless of any personal enmities, "is the conquest of the United States. Northern Maine is French Canadian. In New England we count half a million. Lowell, Worcester, Lawrence, Nashua and Fall River are ours. In farms, in parishes, in solid masses, we shall establish ourselves on the banks of the Merrimac as we have on our own historic streams, to increase and multiply and possess the land, replacing the degenerate New Englander, *possedentes januas hostium*, performing a divine mission, working out a high destiny for our language and the Catholic faith, and establishing a new, magnificent State out of the portions of those destroyed, over which shall fly the lilies of old—"

"And perhaps reign a duly fat Bourbon," interrupted Quinet over his salad.

"We shall re-unite at last again with France! The affection of this remnant of her children, turned adrift in their few arpents of snow, has never died towards the land so changed from the time of our forefathers. It is still to us the Palestine of our speech, our history and our faith of St. Louis! We are the American France!

We are all ready. We are the people of God. In the words of a brother : 'This blood was set in America in the midst of a material world, like France in Europe, to regenerate these peoples and perpetuate the reign of ideals. God has willed it : 'GESTA DEI PER FRANCOS !'"

Chamilly turned to Chrysler as the school master ended, and said with a smile : "Do you not think there is enterprise in a people like this ?"

CHAPTER XVIII.

A DISAPPEARING ORDER.

" Qu'il est triste d'etre vaincu !—"
—Du Calvet.

From Quinet who had been deliberately dealing with his dessert, now came words:

" Mistaken impulses ! Led after will o' the wisps by dreamers and designers ! If it were not that all movements work but one way, like the backward and forward of a machine—towards *advancement,* these things would make a man despond."

" What then, sir," Chrysler asked, " are your ideas ? "

" Hear me, like a different messenger from the same battle. The motto, ' God has made Law to Every Man to Labour,' means that the slaves of priestcraft are to be contented with their servitude. ' To Make the People Better,' means to blind the second eye of their obedience."

" To— ? "

" Stop my dear friend," Chamilly interrupted with emotion, " that motto's words are sacred to me and will ever justly be to all our people. Do not, disparage that motto ? "

" I will never disparage making the people truly better. It is to the tone of those who usurp the aim, you should apply my critique. The men who lip these terms are none other than the evil geniuses of history. It is the *Jesuits* who would make us poor and miserable,—who have wrecked French America, past and future. Without them we should have welcomed to our dominions from the first, an immigration twice larger than England's : we should have held the continent north, south and centre ; our people would have been vitalized by education instead of so ignorant that no commoner but one ever wrote a book ; they would have built and flourished and extended ; and in place of a poor and helpless people they would have been rich, powerful, and self-reliant, like the Bostonians ; Bigot and his nest of horse-leeches would never have sucked our blood and left us to ruin ! "

He paused, but as if not yet quite finished. His hearers listened.

"And *since*—," he suddenly and energetically added, with a stern look around and a bitter suggestiveness on the word as if it were enough to pronounce it ; and in truth, it silenced both De La Lande and Chamilly, and appeared to make a completely effective ending.

In the evening, walking out on the road before retiring, Chamilly and Chrysler commented on the discussion, and Chrysler said, " I must say I was unprepared for this debate. I was a poor helpless Briton, caught like Braddock in Mr. De La Lande's ambush. Tell me what you think yourself of these things."

"It is a sad thing to belong to a disappearing order," Haviland replied, " Sympathising with my people, I am grieved in a sense to believe their present aspirations dreams. It is sad to behold any race, and deeply so if it is your own, blind in the presence of unalterable forces which will soon begin their removal of what it considers to be dearest."

" I sympathize with them and you," Chrysler said.

" Ecclesiasticism ruins us !" exclaimed Quinet the Radical, who was with them :

" Quiconque me résiste et me brave est impie
Ce qu'ici-bas j'écris, là-haut Dieu la copie."

" You should moderate your animosity," Chamilly said. These Jesuits are most certainly humble, self-devoted men ? "

" I detest them as machines, not as men ! " retorted the Radical.

CHAPTER XIX.

HUMAN NATURE.

"Va . . .
A monsieur le Curé
Lui dire que sa paroisse
'Est tout bouleversée."
—Popular Ballad.

Curé L'Archeveque, black skull-cap on head, was in the best of humour, playing with his little dog in the ample reception-room of the parsonage, when a laborer came and brought an account of several late doings in the village.

When Messire heard what had been said at Zotique's, his rotund black stole writhed as if founts of lava boiled in him ; his face swelled to the likeness of a fiery planet ; indignation choked his speech for four minutes by the face of the tall clock in his sitting-room ; and then the lava rose to the surface in jets :

" Gang of accurseds ! "

" Atheists ! "

" Freemasons ! "

He turned for a moment to the laborer again who had come to inform him. Then he exploded successively as before :

" They laughed ? "

" They laughed ! "

" I will make them laugh ! "

The young curé, his vicar, who was present, tried to calm him, but could not.

His energies turned to action; he dismissed the parishioner, who, hat in hand, stood humbly by the door, and sitting down began to write letters and concoct vows.

The first of the latter was to announce a spiritual boycott from the pulpit on Zotique and his iniquitous hall; and with this he wrote to the Attorney-General on the scandal of the gross misuse of the Circuit Court and the bad character of the local Registrar.

The second bitter vow was that the Liberals should lose their election: this inspired a letter to Grandmoulin, the "Cave" Chief.

There were other vows and other letters; one each to the Bishop and the Archbishop,—whose contents are unknown.

At similar times, however, the Reverend gentleman had a recreation to which he was accustomed to turn for refreshment, and this was not long in rising in his mind. By law he was Visitor to the secular school: than which there was nothing he considered more nearly the root of all evil. He therefore took up his brown straw hat and black cane, and started determinedly out to exercise his habit of vexing the high spirit of the school master, De La Lande.

"Ah bon, fratello!" cried Zotique that afternoon when de La Lande appeared at his door, "How goes it? Come in and speak to Mr. Chrysler, here."

"It goes ill, Zotique," answered the school master, gloomily, "I have had the Curé again."

"And what did he say to you?"

"Quarrels with everything in the system. Our geography was galimatias, and book-keeping a crime: the people must not think they were on a level with the learned, and the children must do this and that. At last—at last—I was exasperated, and told him I had a right under the laws to my position and powers. He said there can be no right against the Right! I told him there were many wrongs against the Right! And he went away saying he would bring me to a bed of straw."

"Let him do !" laughed the Registrar.

But Zotique himself was not to escape quite scot-free, for when Chrysler stopped next day at his office, as he was getting accustomed to do, he found him in one of his excitements.

* "Àc-ré-yé !" he was ejaculating.

"Ah, good day, sir. Come in and take a seat. Aa-a-créyé, how they enrage us !"—and he cast an impatient glance on the floor at a large envelope deeply marked with his heel.

"What is the matter ?" Chrysler queried.

"The matter, sir, is that ! "—spurning the envelope.

"An official notification ?"

"Not official ! — No, sir, unofficial ! ultra-official, contra-official, pseud-official ! See, read it ! "

He picked up and handed over the objectionable letter, which was headed with the stamp of the Attorney-General's Office :—"Dear Sir,—You are requested to grant Mr. Cletus Libergent the use of the Circuit Court edifice and rooms, which are in your charge, for whatever purpose he may desire, for the space of three weeks from the present date."

T. OUAOUARON,

Attorney-General."

Chrysler smiled to Zotique. Could a Government that openly granted the public buildings to partisans pretend to a sense of right or dignity ?

As to the effects of the Curé's second vow, they remain matter for narration to come.

---

* Note.—An evasive form of "Sacré," analogous to "Sapré," "Sacristie," "Sac," "St. Christophe," &c.

CHAPTER XX.

CHEZ NOUS.

" Bonjour le maître et la maîtresse
Et tous les gens de la maison."
—The Guignolee Carol.

The crimson and gold of sunset were stained richly across the west. Chrysler was walking leisurely out in the country. A mile from Dormillière, a white stone farm-house stood forward near the road. In front, across the highway, the low cliff swelled out into the stump of a headland, which bore spreading on its grassy top three mighty and venerable oaks.

Chrysler, pondering as was his wont upon this and everything, noting the surges of color in the sky, the clear view, the procession of odd-looking homesteads down the road ; their narrow fields running back indefinitely ; the resting flocks and herds ; here a group of thatched-roof barns, and there a wayside cross ; passed along and mused on the peace of life in this prairie country, and the goodness of the Almighty to His children of every tongue.

The strains of a violin in the farm-house struck his ear. Some-one was fiddling the well-known sprightly air, " Vive la Canadienne : "

" Long live the fair Canadian girl,
With her sweet, tender eyes."

The house was a large cottage, having around its door a slender gallery, at whose side went down a stair. Its chimnies were stout, and walls thick, its roof pitched very steep and clipped off short at the

eaves ; a garden of lilac-bushes and shrubs, some of which pressed
their dark green against its spotless white-wash, surrounding it in
front and on one side, while on the other lay the barn-yard, with a
large wooden cross in its centre, protected by a railing.   Two
hundred years ago such houses were built in Brittany.

Chrysler's glances took in with curiosity the tiny window up in the
gable, the quaint-cut iron bars of the cellar openings, the small-paned
sashes of the four front windows.

Above the door, was the rude-cut inscription:

A Dieu la Gloire

J. B.

1 7 6 8.

The fiddler drew his attention particularly, however, to the people
on the gallery.   There was one at least whom he had seen before.   A
cavalier of much shirt-front and large mouth, and on whose make-up,
Nature had printed "BAR-TENDER" in capitals—in short the
"Spoon" of Zotique's reception—was sitting on the balustrade of the
little gallery, making courtship over the shoulder of a dark-eyed maid,
whose mother—a square-waisted archetype of her—stood in the door.
Paterfamilias sat on the top step with his back to Chrysler, barring
the stair rather awkwardly with his legs.   A second young man
slender, and dressed in a frock coat of black broad-cloth, and silk
hat, and with face pale, but of undiscourageable cheerfulness, though
without doubt repulsed by the father's attitude from a front attack on
the position, was taking the three steps in the garden necessary to
bring him alongside the gallery.   And, unobserved, down beside her
dress, the maiden's fair hand was dropping him a sprig of lilac.

Within, the grandfather bent crooked over his violin.

Our traveller halted, there was a whisper, and the music stopped.

"Salut, Monsieur," cried the householder, stumbling down the steps and hurrying half-way across the garden, where he took up a position, "Monsieur is tired. Will he honour my roof? All here is yours, and I and my family are at your service. Enter, Monsieur."

A dramatic gesture of humility recalled at once the man in blue homespun, who had addressed the crowd at Zotique's.

"Good evening, Mr. Benoit," the Ontarian said, opening the gate and mustering his French, "I shall be charmed."

The air immediately bustled with hospitality.

"Come in, sir, come in," feebly rasped the voice of the old man from the door. "Josephte, bring a chair for Monsieur." "I will fetch one!" cried the good-wife. The girl Josephte, rose from her seat and followed her mother quickly into the house; the pale young man in the garden doubled his cheerful smile; and only the bar-tender endued himself in an aggressive grin of independence.

"I assure you, monsieur," pronounced Jean Benoit, with his full armory of oratorical gestures, "that a friend of Monseigneur Chamilly will always have our best. Ascend, sir.—Josephte, place Monsieur the chair."

Never was there a greater occasion of state.

Their guest raised his hat to the young lady and her mother, who threw into her carriage all the dignity and suavity she could command. Then he ascended and sat gratefully down, for he was fatigued.

The grandfather had laid his instrument on a spinning-wheel within the door, and slowly lit a pipe with both hands. The bar-tender jumped from his perch and stood with a familiar leer, of which when Benoit said "Mr. Cuiller, monsieur," Chrysler took trifling notice. On the other hand the pale lover remained modestly down the steps, and his cheerfulness redoubled when Chrysler nodded to him, passingly introduced as "Le Brun."

" Does the gentleman take white whiskey,* or well milk ?" asked the
old man. " Josephte, bring some milk."

The daughter darted into the house.—" There is tea on the
stove, Josephte !" Madame called hurriedly inwards, "and bring out
some cakes and apples, and perhaps Monsieur would like new honey.
—Be comfortable, sir."

" Monsieur has come into the parish for the election ?" the old man
queried politely.

" Only to see what passes," he replied, accepting the bowl of milk
which Josephte tendered him, and a piece of raisin cake from a
pile on a blue-pattern plate.—" What do you think of it ?"

But a diversion occurred. The wife had retired a few moments, and
a veteran piano commenced playing, while a spirited boy's voice struck
up a hymn from the services of the Church,—" O Salutaris Hostia."
It was her youngest son, whom she had not been able to resist showing
off a little. Chrysler praised the voice, which was excellent, and the
boy, attired in a neat, black, knee-breeches suit with white stockings,
was proudly brought forward and presented.

The grandfather had the twinkle in his eye of a true country violinist.

" I was going to tell them a story of the old times, sir. Will you
pardon me ?" he said, with the twinkle sparkling.

Chrysler protested his own desire to listen.

" We always like to hear about the old times," said young Le Brun,
apologetically.

" It's about a rascality of Zotique's, the droll boy, when we
were young—the delectable history of Mouton. Mouton, the servant
of Pére Galibert, who in those times was Curé, was a fat man, of the
air of a tallow image. You know Legros—the butcher's son,—just
like that. If he had had red hair there would have been spontaneous
combustion."

* Highwines.

"Someone stole the sacramental wine of Père Galibert, and every-one except the Père knew it was Mouton. Messire would never believe them, though it so angered him he preached fourteen discourses against the thief. They were eloquent sermons."

"One Sunday afternoon—it was about the Day of St. Michel, when we went in to pay the seigneur his rents—Zotique was at the presbytère with me and his brother, the Honorable, and all of us playing cards with Père Galibert. Zotique had come down from the city with a new keg of wine for the Sacrament, and they were discussing the disappearance. Mouton was there, and he says never a word. "Let it alone," says Zotique, and he looks around and takes up the inkbottle carelessly from the shelf and goes off to the kitchen and down into the cellar, where he puts away the wine, and then he comes back to us, upstairs. Mouton disappears in a moment. Zotique pretends to play, but he is calculating the seconds. Presently he says, "Monsieur le Curé, you and I are too good players. Let Mouton take my place, and do you play against Benoit and my cousin," and without waiting for any answer he flies out to the kitchen, and cries sharply : "Mouton, Messire wants you !" adding, "Quick, quick, tête de Mouton !" Mouton rushes upstairs, brushing his mouth. There he stands before us, solid as the image of tallow ; but his mouth was as black as an oven's, *and his features indistinguishable with ink.*"

The circle, all eagerly listening, burst forth :

"How did Zotique do it ?" they cried.

"Voila the mystery."

"What was done to Mouton ?"

"Père Galibert boiled him down into tapers, and sold him to the congregation."

The old man put his pipe, which had gone out, once more to

his lips and nonchalantly repeated the operation of lighting it between his hands.

Spoon, his low felt hat tipped over his eyes made Josephte blush crimson with his attentions. Her glances and smiles were to François.

Chrysler as he watched her, saw that it was she whose spiritual expression had attracted him at church. Near at hand, he took notes of her appearance. She was of modest face, regular and handsome in features, though not striking, and her cheek wore just a suggestion of color. Dressed in black, her apparel and demeanor were quietly perfect.

The fine sweep of view from the gallery across the water attracted him, and his eyes rested upon the leafy monarchs shadowing the river-bank before them.

" Your house is well placed," he said in admiration.

" Yes, Monsieur," replied the old man, simply, and he pointed out the various parishes whose spires could be descried across the water.

Thus conversing and observing, the Ontarian spent an instructive and delightful hour. When he rose to go, calm and rested, the hospitality again became profuse. " The gentleman will not walk ! " shrilly protested highly-pleased mater familias. " Go François," turning to young Le Brun : " row Monsieur to the Manoir, you and Mr. Cuiller. Take the rose *chaloupe*, and Josephte shall go too."

Chrysler made a very admirable guest. He would have struck you as a fine, large man, of kindly face, and influential manner, and people pressed upon him their best wherever he went. " You speak our tongue, sir," said the grandfather, " That is a great thing. I have often thought that if all the people of the earth spoke but one speech they would all be brothers. What an absurdity to be divided by mere syllables."

So they parted, with many " Au revoirs " and mutual compliments

at the water-side   The willing François planted one foot on a stone
in the water and handed the young lady into the boat, and Cuiller
hastening for the seat next her, made a pretended accidental lunge of
his heavy shoulder at him into the water.   François kept his balance
and, quite unconscious of the malicious stratagem, held the ill-
wisher himself from going over, which he almost did, to Josephte's
demure amusement; next Chrysler got in and Francois essayed to
push off.   But as the boat stuck in the bottom and refused to
stir, he suddenly dropped his hold, and with an "Avance donc!"
gallantly slushed his way into the water alongside, in his Sunday
trousers, lifted the gunwale and started her afloat, amidst a shower of
final "Au revoirs," and the rose *chaloupe* moved with noiseless
smoothness down the current.   •

Peace reigned over every surrounding.   The broad, molten-like
surface; the dusky idealizing of the lines of cottages and delicate
silhouetting of the trees along the shore near them; the artistic
picture of the old white farm-house, mystic-looking in the soft
evening light, with its shapes of lilac-trees rioting about it and
the three great oaks darkening the bank in front; the ghost of light
along the distant horizon; the gentle coolness of the air; the
occasional far-off echo of some cry; and the regular splash and
gleam of the oars as they leave the water or dip gently in again.
A fish leaps.   An ocean steamer, low in the distance, can be descried
creeping noiselessly on.   The islands and shores mirror themselves
half-distinctly in the water.

A mile above, some boatful of pensive hearts are singing.   So calm
is the evening that the cadences come distinctly to us, and almost the
words can be plainly caught.   In a lull of their song, faint sounds of
another arrive from far away.   Rising and falling, now heard and
now not, plaintive and recurring, it is like the voices of spirits.

But farther, farther yet, a still more distant echo—a suggestion

scarcely real—floats also to us. The whole river, in its length and
breadth, from Soulanges and the Lake of Two Mountains, and the
tributary Ottawa, to Quebec and Kamouraska and the shores of
the Gulf beyond, all is alive with plaintive sweetness, echoing
from spirit to spirit, (for it is a fiction that music is a thing of
lips and ears), old accents of Normandy, Champagne, and Angoulême.

The brimming François strikes up by natural suggestion of his
dipping oars;

" A la claire fontaine
M'en allant promener."

I.

" Beside the crystal fountain
     Turning for ease to stray,
So fair I found the waters
     My limbs in them I lay.
                         Long is it I have loved thee,
                             Thee shall I love alway,
                                      My dearest.
                         Long is it I have loved thee,
                             Thee shall I love alway.

II.

So fair I found the waters,
     My limbs in them I lay :
Beneath an oak tree resting,
     I heard a roundelay.
                    Long is it, &c.

III.

Beneath an oak tree resting,
     I heard a roundelay,
The nightingale was singing
     On the oak tree's topmost spray.
                    Long is it, &c.

IV.

The nightingale was singing
     On the oak tree's topmost spray :—

Sing, nightingale, keep singing,
  Thou who hast heart so gay !
    Long is it, &c.

V.

Sing, nightingale, keep singing,
  Thou hast a heart so gay,
Thou hast a heart so merry,
  While mine is sorrow's prey.
    Long is it, &c.

VI.

For I have lost my mistress,
  Whom I did true obey,
All for a bunch of roses,
  Whereof I said her nay.
    Long is it, &c.

VII.

I would those luckless roses,
  Were on their bush to-day,
And that itself the rosebush
  Were plunged in ocean's spray.
    Long is it I have loved thee,
    Thee shall I love alway,
      My dearest
    Long is it I have loved thee,
    Thee shall I love alway.

The melody was of a quiet, haunting strangeness, and from the end of the words "Thou who hast heart so gay," the maiden perfected it by interweaving an exquisite contralto into the chorus,

    Long is it I have loved thee,
    Thee shall I love alway.

In this fashion was Chrysler delivered at the Manoir, and when Chamilly asked him "Where have you been this evening?" as he entered the grounds, he answered, "In Arcadia !"

CHAPTER XXI.

DELIVER US FROM THE EVIL ONE.

"Aïe ! cela ressemble un peu à certaine fable célèbre, dont la morale se résume à ceci : ne comptez pas sans votre hôte."

—BENJAMIN SULTE.

"St. Gregory the Great ! Here comes the Small-pox !" exclaimed Zotique, as he and Chamilly, with their guest, were off behind the Manoir, and standing by the weather-worn Chapel in the hay-fields, which served as the tomb of the first Haviland, " the Pro-testant Seigneur."

The name "Picault" offered itself so readily to the pun of "Picotte,"—Small-pox,—that the jest had become almost a usage.

Startled by Zotique's exclamation, Mr. Chrysler looked from the commemorative table on the Chapel's side (whose rivulet of eulogies he was reading line by line), towards the pine-walk round the Manoir, whence a distant figure was sauntering towards them along the path, meditatively smoking a cigar.

" That's a fact," exclaimed Chamilly, straining his eyes towards the figure ; and the three looked at each other in astonishment. " Has he actually the enterprise to try me again ? Or what can he want ? "

" I can answer you," the veracious Zotique undertook, " my eyes are good.—He is smiling fully a second hundred thousand."

" That is courage after what I gave him for the first."

" It is doubtless, then, glory :—say Member of the Council."

" Did I ever tell you of the last time he came to me, and offered not only that Membership, but finally advanced to the Presidency of it. Imagine the recklessness of the Province's interests—A President of the Council at twenty-four years! More than that, if I wished for active glory, he would give either the local Premiership, or undertake to combine the French parties at Ottawa, and put me at their head, with a surety of being Premier of the whole country. And this again for a youth of twenty-four years!—He tried to flatter me that I was a Pitt or a Napoleon. And I answered, that no man guilty of such a compact could be either."

" You will do it without him," replied Zotique, confidently.

Chrysler looked closely at the approaching figure, growing larger and clearer.

" Where is he Member for ? " he asked.

" Member for Hoang-ho *in partibus infidelium*," replied Zotique, sarcastically.

Picault sauntered up with a smile of unfaltering genial sang-froid, bowed, removed his cigar, and addressed them.

" Salut, my dear Haviland, salut Messieurs. Oh! my dear Genest, how goes it?" offering his hand, which Zotique took with a caricature of extravagant joy and imitation of the other's style :

" My dear Small-pox—pardon me—my dear friend, I am charmed to meet again a man of so much sense and honor."

" Ah yes, we have fought on many a field, but we respect each other. ' Honneur au plus vaillant.' But why, my dear Haviland," turning, " why should the valiant oppose each other, and half of them lose at each battle ? Is it not because they are divided ? Union makes strength ! "

" Yes, it is because they are divided by impassable gulfs," said Chamilly, coldly. " Did you come to see me, Monsieur?"

" My dear fellow, can't we have a little private conversation

G

together?   I am, of course, in the country to oppose your politics,
but being in Dormillière, I cannot forget our social acquaintanceship."

"Do me the honor of saying here what you desire to say, Monsieur.
I have no political secrets from these friends."

"Pardon me, what I have to tell you, is strictly private."

"If it is in political matters, I do not wish it to be so."

"It is personal, I assure you."

"Then you will humor me, sir, by writing it."

"My friend, do not let party differences put grimaces at each other
on our real faces :—I would say rather party names ; for I am in
reality as much a Red as yourself. If you were willing we would
prove that to you by changing the title of our side to yours."

"At that moment, sir, there would be what I live for in the name
'Blue.'"

Picault drew a deliberative puff at his cigar, and lowered it again.

"You will not, then, do me the honor of a personal interview?" he
asked, smiling unprovokably still.

"Cease, cease ! replied Haviland, "It will soon be the noon of plain
words !"

The tempter with nice discernment, perceiving that this short and
bold interview was useless, and that he ought to withdraw, put
his cigar between his lips, puffed a "Good-day, gentlemen," and
turned back meditatively, along the path towards the pines of the
Manoir.

"Au plaisir !" returned Zotique to him with facetious exactitude.

Haviland was furious.

"Shall the children of these men, enriched perhaps and elevated
through their crimes," he exclaimed, "pretend in time to come that
they obtained their 'Honorables,' and Knighthoods, and seats on the
Bench of Justice, and of Cabinets fairly from their country, and were

the world's great and true ? Forbid it, and forbid that their names should live except in memory of their paltriness ! "

"But dear Mr. Chrysler," he added in a moment, "you must not take us for party bigots. The masses of the Bleus are honest, and any day our own name may be desecrated by a clique of knaves, our principles represented by the other name."

CHAPTER XXII.

THE MANUFACTORY OF REFLECTIONS.

Haviland's approaching election kept him very busy from this time forward, and deluged him with interviews, canvasses, meetings, great and little, and perpetual calls on his attention. His conscientiousness made him work almost unremittingly, for he determined his part in the struggle to be far more than a matter of mere verbiage and smiles. Mr. Chrysler, like a sensible fellow-Member, quite comprehended the situation, and was content to note the admirable way in which his friend did everything; to receive a smile or friendly direction here and there, and to fall back on the attentions of l'Honorable, and the over-zealous Zotique. He felt his entry free, however, to the office where Haviland was principally employed, and which was not uninteresting of itself. There the young man had gathered a library of statistical volumes and other statesman's lore, with busts of Thiers and Cæsar and strangely ideal and unlike the rest,—a pure white classic mask of Minerva on the wall opposite his chair, as if to strike the note of a higher life; while Brebœuf, curious little object, devoured some blue-book in a corner.

Now what were those great aims of Haviland's? NATION-MAKING, we know in general. But what was the work upon which he was employed as the means?

On the occasion of one of Chrysler's quiet entries, Haviland rose from his table as the light began to fall, threw off his toils with a breath of relief, and turning towards the older gentleman, called his attention to a large green tin case of pigeon-holes and drawers of different sizes, labelled.

" Here," he said, " is my manufactory of reflections."

One compartment was marked " FINANCES," another " LABOUR," a small one " DEFENCE," and a drawer lying open for use was titled " THE UNITY OF RACES."

" Take out a paper, Mr. Chrysler."

Chrysler put forth his hand willingly, and withdrawing one, held it to the window and read as follows :

" A great thought can be thought in any place. A great Empire may be planned in any corner."

The second was a note from " GENERAL NEEDS."

" What the country most requires is Devoted Men."

Others read similarly, some long, some short.

" I can show you what will strike you more," exclaimed Chamilly, in a moment. " I have been planning your visit a little."

" Have you a geyser or a catacomb ?"

" No sir,—a fountain of life," replied he, jocosely. " Let us get our hats."

CHAPTER XXIII.

THE STATESMAN'S DREAM.

As they went down the village, he continued to banter.

"You great Ontarians believe too firmly that there is no progress here. According to you there is no being to be met in these forsaken wastes, except a superstitious peasant, clothed all the year in 'beefs' and homespun, capped with the tuque, girded with the sash, and carrying the capuchin hood on his shoulders, like the figure on some of our old copper *sous ;*—who sows, after the manner of his fathers, a strip of the field of his grandfathers, and cherishes to his heart every prejudice of his several great, great-grandfathers."

"I do not think so," interrupted Chrysler laughing, "I might put you fifty years behind the age, but no further."

"Yes, but you, sir, have seen us. Why do not more of you come and see ?"

"For some of the same reasons perhaps why you do not know us."

Some distance past the Church northward, the village, obscured by the great, irregularly-occurring pines, takes a turn and a sudden dip. The dip and the pines, which are thick at that end, obscure a section of the village known locally as La Reveillière.

As they came to the high ground where the dip occurs, the vista appeared below of a spacious avenue, down whose centre ran a straight and smooth road-bed, and on either side twice its breadth of lawn, rolled and cut, forming a sort of common, ornamented by a sparing group or two of the ubiquitous pines of the neighbourhood. Along the edges of this avenue or common, lay what could only be called a sort of *transfigured French-Canadian village*, looking, in the quiet light of evening, as if pictured by some artist out of studies of the places in the country about. The dwellings were larger, better drawn, their windows, attics and wings more varied in design, but amid their picturesque variety could be discerned in several, a suggestion of the chimney of a certain wild little cot in a dell near the Manoir; in others, of the solid stone home of Jean Benoit; in many the châlet-eaved pattern of the ordinary cottage. Perhaps the latter were made prettiest of all—they were at least the airiest looking. It was in the colors and stainings applied to the gables and other parts that the greatest care had been taken. These were selected out of the ordinary red, yellow, white, and sage-green washes in common use, with such taste as to effect a deeply harmonious and ideal issue. Again, the plan of the village was peculiar. It was simply an improvement on that of the local villages in general, the dwellings being upon the border of the street and not far apart, with their little, foot-wide flower-gardens close against the front. The circular fan of a patent windmill lifted itself lightly, the most prominent object in the settlement, and a charming Gothic schoolhouse crouched farther down on the opposite side. Behind the houses, growths of trees formed an enclosing background, according to the tastes of the owners, but guided by some harmonizing supervision like the colors. And at a short distance the avenue was crossed by a white poplar grove, which brought the scene to a limit, and separated this dream of a rural statesman from the common world.

"V'là, monsieur," said Zotique, who had joined them, stretching his hand, "Behold the cherished work of our young seigneur."

Upon the galleries, the verandahs, the green lawn, the picture moved with life. A half-haze, precursive of the twilight, lent scenic softness to the forms of old men puffing their pipes before the doors, a maiden listlessly strolling on the sward, a swarm of children playing

near the road, a distant toiler making his way home, bearing his
scythe.   The visitors went down into the place and Chrysler saw that
the artistic shapes and ideal colors were worn with daily use, the men
and women, serene-looking, were still the every day mortals of the
region.

"I think I have gained a great step in the houses and street," said
Haviland.

"And the Reveillière is proud of its founder," added l'Honorable.

"We have a little newspaper—*Le Coup d'Œil.*"—cried Zotique.

Chrysler congratulated Chamilly on his felicity of design in the
dwellings.

The greater size of the houses was chiefly for better ventilation.
The windmill was part of a simple water-works system, which
supplied the village with draughts from the bottom of the river.
The school was a gift of Chamilly's.

"If we had some great architect among us," replied he, "he would
transmute for our country a national architecture."

A little house, conspicuous for the delicacy of its architecture, stood
near them, and a young man—the schoolmaster—who was on the
verandah, reading, in his shirtsleeves, threw down his newspaper at the
call of Zotique, came forward and entered eloquently into the work of
information about the Reveillière, flinging his cotton-clad arms
recklessly towards the winds of heaven.

"The Institute—the fountain of all—the gentleman has not seen
the Institute?" inquired he, looking to the two Frenchmen.

"I believe not," Zotique said.   "Have you seen it, sir?"

"Not that I know of."

"Monsieur, you must see the Institute."

"What is this Institute?"

"The *enfant perdu* of Liberalism, the mainspring of Dormillière,
the hope of French America!"

CHAPTER XXIV.

THE INSTITUTE.

" The battle for the sway,
Of liberty,
Fraternity,
And light of the new day."
—MARY MORGAN.

"About eighteen hundred and fifty," explained the Honorable, " L'Institut Canadien was our national thinking Society, and the spark of an awakening of great promise."

"Under the French regime, our people received no education. They knew the forests, the rapids, the science of trapping beaver, and when to expect the Iroquois, and sow grain. The English conquest came next and cut us off from the new birth of modern France, and the Church, our only institution, was very willing to ignore that stimulation of ideas. We lived on ; we read little ; we labored much.—But, monsieur," said l'Honorable, with his quiet dignity, " we were of the race of Descartes."

" We slept. At last the awakening ! Our griefs and our grievances forced the Rebellion ; they brought our thoughts together and made us reason in common ; we demanded a new Canada, relieved of bureaucracy, of political disabilty, of seignioral oppression, some said even of abuses of the Church—a Canada of the People, in which every citizen should stand up equal and free.

" The first result demanded—and obtained—was responsible government. Among others came preparations for the abolition of feudal tenure, making a vassal population freeholders !

"The next cry was Education! The French-Canadians were delighted with the opening world of knowledge and ideas, and there is no race which ever rose with greater enthusiasm to pursue progress and science. A few young men of Montreal were banded into a Society for mutual advancement, to hold debates at which all races were to be free to contribute opinions, to open a library of useful books, and to seek truth without any conditions. That was the Institut Canadien!

"These noble young enthusiasts soon attracted chosen spirits, a precious essence of the race. They sprang into fame;—fourteen were returned to Parliament in one year. They called all the world freely to their discussions, and created éclat by the brilliancy of their programme. The province kindled—every village had its Institute!"

"But 'sa-a-a-cr!'" savagely ejaculated Zotique, and his eyes grew intense in their fierceness.

"The Institut Canadien gradually excited the jealousy of certain ecclesiastics by its free admissions and the liberality of its researches. What is known as the "Struggle" commenced. A series of combined assaults by episcopal summons, a pulpit crusade, excommunication, refusal of burial, encouragement of dissensions, and the establishment of rival Institutes bearing names such as "Institut Canadien Français," most of which existed only on paper, finally succeeded in crushing the movement.

"Ac"—ejaculated Zotique.

"The Institute at Dormillière is the insignificant sole survivor."

"I understand now your Reveillière," Chrysler said.

CHAPTER XXV.

THE CAMPAIGN PLAN.

On Saturday evening of Chrysler's first week at the Manoir, they went to the Institute. It was a house down the Dormillière Street, that held its head somewhat higher and tipped it back a little more proudly than the rest,—a long, old fashioned wooden cottage, of many windows, and some faded pretensions to the ornamental : still elegant in the light curve of its capacious grey roof, the slender turned pillars of its gallery, separated by horizontal oval arches, its row of peaked and moulded dormer windows, its ornaments, its broad staircase climbing up to the doorway, and the provincial-aristocratic look of its high set-back position in its garden. The name of a rich money-lender, who had been feared in days gone by—"Cletus the Ingrate,"—was mentioned under breath in the stories about it. But ever since his death, many years before, it had been the faded outer shell into which the intellectual kernel of Dormillière life withdrew itself, and in the passage as one entered, the sign "INSTITUT CANADIEN," which had once had its place on the front, might be seen resting on the floor,—a beehive and the motto "Altius Tendimus," occupying the space between the two words.

The interior was a very great contrast to the outside. Its fittings were in the pleasantest of light-hued paints and varnished pine : maps, casts, and pictures enlivened the walls and corners ; a handsome library and nucleus of a museum, with reading tables, opened to the left, and a large debating hall to the right—together occupying the whole of the principal floor.

That evening the row of front windows shone with particular illumination for a meeting of Chamilly's supporters, and as Chrysler entered with Haviland and Zotique, they caught from De La Lande the fragmentary assertion, " It is France that must be preached ! "

" Aux armes, citoyens ! " roared Zotique, entering like a captain on the stage. " Give me my battalion ! Write me my letters of marque : " Then throwing one hand in air : " Allons ! what has been done ? "

The audience sitting around on tables and windowsills, as well as on groups of chairs, laughed boisterously and thumped the floor, and recalled to the proper work of the meeting, commenced a cry of " l'Honorable ! "

" The Honorable presides ! " intoned Benoit, like a crier ; and Genest, accustomed to understand their wishes, seated himself in the chair, while a momentary lull fell over the noisiness.

" A Secretary ! "

" De La Lande ! "

" Calixte Lefebvre ! "

" Le Brun, Le Brun, Le Brun, Le Brun ! "

" I nominate our good friend Descarries," smilingly spoke the Chairman. " Does the meeting agree ? "

" Yes ! " " Yes ! " " Maitre Descarries for Secretary ! " " Maitre Descarries ! " " Carried ! " were the responses shouted together from all sides.

" We have to consider this evening," continued the Chairman, after the white-wigged official had seated himself in his place as Secretary, " our general organization and appointment of districts. The aim is to work hard for Monsieur during the times coming. The people's meeting to take place to-morrow, is to be addressed for Libergent by Grandmoulin himself, and Picault will be in the county with them till the election. So you see our task is not less than to defeat the whole strength of the Cave.　As we fight with men of stature, there is need of valor and address."

"We'll have to pull the devil by the tail!" cried one.　The words were those of a common proverb referring to "close shaving."

The Chairman added : "Mr. De La Lande, the floor seems to be already yours."

"I have heard," began De La Lande, "that Grandmoulin has commenced to raise the issue of French patriotism."

"You are right," said Zotique.

"Well, then, why can we not use a like word, that shall go to the heart of the people ?　Give us a national cry !　Let the struggle rest on our fundamental emotions of race !　Why can we not"—The face of the impetuous schoolmaster began to flame into eagerness and fire.

"Because," interrupted Haviland, firmly, "we are in this particular country.　Would you have us enter upon a campaign of injustice and ill-will ?　Leave that, and the glory of it, to Grandmoulin and to Picault ! "

"But, my chief, the positions of the French and the English !—We who were first, are becoming last ! "

"Come here if you please, sir," Haviland said, turning to Chrysler, who rose and advanced to him surprised.　Haviland took him, and passing over to De La Lande, placed the hand of the Ontario gentleman in that of the high-spirited schoolmaster, who accepted it, puzzled. "There ! " cried Haviland, raising his voice to a pitch of solemnity. "Say whatever you can in that position.　*That is the position of the Canadian races ?* "

A shout rose in the hall, and every man sprang to his feet.　Cheer rose upon cheer, while De La Lande shook the hand in his with feeling ; and the cheering, smiling, and hand shaking, lasted nearly a minute.

It ended at a story by Zotique.

"When I was a boy,"—he began, in a deep, exaggerated voice, and whirling his two arms so as to include the whole of those present in the circle of his address. The cheers and confusion broke into a roar of laughter for a moment, that stifled itself almost as quickly, as they listened.

"We lived for a year in the Village Ste. Aldegonde, near to Montreal. In the Village Ste. Aldegonde there was a nation of boys. All these boys marched in daily to town to the great School of the Blessed Brothers. Along the way to the School of the Blessed Brothers, many English boys lay in wait between us and learning, and we passed certain streets like Hurons passing through the forests of Iroquois. Often we went in large war parties, and repeated the charges of Waterloo for hours up and down streets

"One afternoon I passed there alone—accompanied by a great boaster. We behold three big English boys. We cross the street. They come after :—get before us :—command us to stop !"

The audience were worked up into suppressed fits, for Zotique's gestures were inimitable.

"My friend the boaster steps forward with the air Napoleonic ! He sticks out his breast like this ; he shortens his neck, like this ; he frowns his brows ; he glares at them a terrible look ; he cries : 'I am of the Canadian blood !' "

"And what does he do next, gentlemen ?" Zotique paused a moment.

—"Runs for his life ! "

The roar that followed shook the apartment. Zotique stopped it.

"But what did _I_ do, gentlemen ?"

No one ventured to guess.

"I—perhaps because I was of the Dormillière blood—did not run, but looked at the English.—We laughed all together.—And I passed along unmolested."

"Messieurs,—with the exception of our excellent De La Lande, I am afraid it is too often those who lack the virtues of their race who make most cry of it."

The meeting now resumed its discussions.

"We require strategy!" asserted a burly, red-haired lawyer from the City.

"I confess myself in favor of strategy," admitted Zotique also.

"I am always in favor," said Chamilly, "of the strategy of organized tactics, of the avoidance of useless by-questions, and of spirit and intelligence in attack and defence."

"But you will not let us lie a little in protection of you," retorted Zotique. "To me the moral law is to beat Picault."

"Assuredly!" the red-haired lawyer said indignantly, looking a half air of patronage towards Chamilly, and breathing in for a steady blast of eloquence : "It is time these ridiculous ideas which forbid us so many successes were sent back to Paradise, and that such elections as the present were governed upon rational principles. We cannot offer the people directly what is good for them ; because it is not what they want. What they want, is what we must first of all assume to provide. Once in power we can persuade them afterwards. Gentlemen, *to get into power* is the first absolute necessity. We cannot defeat the enemy except by opposing to them some of their own methods. Revive the courage of the young men by offering what they deserve—good places in case of success! Replenish the coffers by having our army of contractors to oppose to the ranks of theirs. If they lie, we have a right to lie. If they spend money, we must spend it. If they cajole with figures, surely our advantage as to the facts would enable us to produce others still more astonishing. Human nature is not angelic—and you can never make it otherwise."

"My friend," answered Chamilly, raising his strong frame deliberately, "these are the very principles that I am resolutely determined to battle with all my forces, I care not whether among my foes or my friends. Must our young Liberals learn over again what Liberalism is? The true way to enter politics is none other at any time than to deliberately choose a higher stand and methods. Trickeries are easier and sometimes lead to a kind of success : if our objects were sordid, we might descend to demeaning hypocrisies, we might cheat, we might thieve, perjure, and be puppets, and perhaps so win our way to power ; we might think we could use these to better ends, though that doctrine succeeds but rarely ;—and perhaps what we might achieve may appear to you of some value, even of great value to you.

"Yet, no, my friends of Dormillière, your very work is to lay the foundations of sincerity deep in this sphere, and to withstand and eradicate the existing political evils. 'One must determine,' said a very great man, 'to serve the people and not to please them.' If some youth replies, 'This is a laborious, troublesome, hopeless occupation, in which there is not reward enough to make it worth my while,' I tell him but 'Attack it : rejoice to see something so near to challenge your mettle, and if you meet the battle boldly so, and ennoble yourself, you will immediately understand how to think of the ennoblement of your people and your country as glorious.' '*Altius tendimus*! We move towards a higher !'—The country reads our motto, and is watching what we practise. Give it an answer in all your acts ! "

Chamilly's manner of uttering these words produced the only perfect stillness the meeting observed during the evening, for the French-Canadians have a custom of talking among themselves throughout any ordinary debate. Their respect for Chamilly was striking. L'Honorable listened with a smile of pleasure ; Zotique looked all loyalty : and the young men beamed their over-flowing

flowing endorsation of sentiments worthy of the Vigers, Dorions, and Papineaus, those grand men whose portraits hung upon their walls.

As he stopped, there was a sudden movement all about. A spirit of energy took hold on all. Zotique, posing at the head of a large table in front of the Chair, almost at once had installed De La Lande assistant-secretary, to do the real work of which punctilious old Maître Descarries could only make a courageous show ; had swept towards him an inkstand, shaken open a drawer and whipped out some foolscap, and darting his cadaverous eyes from one to another around, despotically appointed them to places of various service, now sharply answering, now ignoring a question by the appointee, while De La Lande scribbled his directions ; and everyone was so anxious to find some post that there was no grumbling at his heedless good generalship. In a trice they were all being called for at various tables and corners, which he fixed for the operations of the Committees.

The most zealous and loquacious of those who pressed forward to be given positions of trust was Jean Benoit.

" What pig will you shear ? " demanded Zotique, (looking for an instant, as he turned to shout towards another quarter, " En'oyez donc ; en'oyez ! ")

" I take the Reveillière."

" The Reveillère is parted among three."—(" Be quiet there ! ")

" Well then,"—grandiloquently,—" I take from St. Jean de Dieu to the parish Church of Dormillière."

"Too much for four ! " pronounced Zotique.

Spoon pressed heavily behind Benoit, and whispered something.

" La Misericorde then," said Benoit, hastily.

Zotique shouted to the Secretary : "Jean Benoit the country-side of La Misericorde ! " And to Benoit again :

" There is your committee."

But Jean would have a hand in shoving forward his admired bartender : "Give monsieur something near my own."

"Cuiller—the village of La Misericorde," directed Zotique. "Now, both of you, the chief thing you have to do is to report to us if the Bleus commence to work there. Go ; go!"

"Salut, Benoit ; how goes it ; how is the wife ? and the father ?—the children also ? I hope you are well. Comment ça-va-t-il Cuiller ?" —asked Chamilly.

Spoon took the proffered hand with his sleepy grin. Benoit responded by an obsequiously graceful shaking and deliberative loquacity :

"Well ; well, Monsieur the Seigneur,—We are very well. The wife is well, the father, the children also. And how is Madame the Seigneuresse ? and yourself ? The crisis approaches, does it not ? Eh bien, at that point you will find Jean Benoit strong enough. I have a good heart, Monseigneur. Once Xiste Brin said to me, 'Monsieur the Director, you have a good heart.' Deign to accept my professions, monseigneur, of a loyalty the most solemn, of a breast for ever faithful."

"I have always accepted your friendship, Benoit, and trusted you," smiled generous Haviland. "See here, Zotique, give Benoit a responsible post.—How different must be our feelings at this priceless service of personal affection from those of our opponents, served only for money."

"No money ?" blurted Spoon. "Taurieu ! An election without money ?"

Chamilly, with one quiet glance, turned away to l'Honorable.

"Without 'tin,'—St. Christophe, I say !—St. Laurent !"

"Keep quiet—silence, I pray thee," returned Benoit, and drew his companion aside.

"Why did Benoit call himself Director ?" Chrysler asked.

Haviland and the Honorable smiled : Chamilly answered :

"It is a weakness of his ever since he was put on the Board of our Agricultural Society. Do not laugh, unless at the common vanity of mankind."

CHAPTER XXV.

THE LOW-COUNTRY SUNRISE.

"Chacun son goût. Moi, j'aime mieux la nature primitive qui n'est pas à la mode du jour
mais que l'on ne pourra jamais démoder......J'aime ce que j'aime, et vous, vous aimez autre
chose. Grand bien vous fasse—je vous admire, Monsieur Tout-le-Monde."
—BENJ. SULTE

" I am going to rise before the sun to-morrow. Would you like to
come out fishing ?" remarked Haviland, cheerfully, on the way home.
Chrysler signified assent.

At grey dawn, before it was yet quite daybreak, they were on
the road. All the houses in the neighbourhood looked asleep.
Heavy dews lay upon the grass. The scene was chilly, and a little
comfortless and suggestive of turning back to bed.

" Where are we going ?" the visitor asked, trying to collect his
spirits.

" To find Bonhomme Le Brun, who superintends the boating
interest.—' Bonhomme '—' Good Man '—is a kind of jocular name we
give to every simple old fellow. ' Le Brun ' is not quite correct
either. His real name—or rather the only one extant among the
noms-de-guerre of his predecessors, is Vadeboncœur—' Go willingly,'
which the Notaries I suppose would write ' Vadeboncœur *dit* Le
Brun.' "

Notwithstanding the early hour they were not alone on the road.
A wrinkled woman, bent almost double, was toiling slowly along with
heavy sighs, under a sack of firewood.

" See here, madame," Chamilly called out, stepping forward to her, "give me the sack;" which he unloaded from her back and threw over his shoulder.

" You are always so good, monseigneur Chamilly," the old woman groaned in a plaintive, palsied voice, without straightening her doubled frame.

" Is the Bonhomme at the house ?" he enquired.

" I think not, sir; he was preparing to go to Isle of Ducks."

"Just where I thought," exclaimed Haviland in English. " This Le Brun is of the oddest class—a secular hermit on the solitudes of the river—a species of mystery to the others. Sometimes he is seen paddling among the islands far down; sometimes seining a little by methods invented by himself; sometimes carrying home an old gun and more or less loaded with ducks; sometimes his torch is seen far out in the dark, night-fishing; but few meet him face to face besides myself. When a boy I used to think he lived on the water because his legs were crooked, though more probably his legs are crooked because he avoids the land. He keeps my sail-boat for me and I let him use the old windmill we shall come to by those trees."

The windmill and the cot of Le Brun stood in a birch-grown hollow, not far off, where a stream cascaded into the St. Lawrence, and had worn down the precipitous bank of earth. It was a wild picture. The gable of the cot was stained Indian red down to the eaves, and a stone chimney was embedded irregularly in its log side. The windmill, towering its conical roof and rusty weathervane a little distance off, and stretching out its gray skeleton arms as if to creak more freely in the sweep of gales from the river, was one of those rembrandtesque relics which prove so picturesquely that Time is an artist inimitable by man. A clay oven near the cot completed this group of erections, around and behind which the silver birches and young elms grew up and closed.

H

No, Messieurs, Le Brun was not at home ; he had gone to Isle of Ducks ; and all the blessings of the saints upon Monseigneur for his kindness to a poor old woman.—" Ah, Seigneur ! "

Chamilly took his skiff from the boathouse himself, and was soon pulling swiftly from the shore, while as they got out upon it the vastness and power of the stream became apparent.

From its broad surface the mists began to rise gracefully in long drifts, moved by the early winds and partly obscuring the distant shores, whose fringe of little shut up houses still suggested slumber.   The dews had freshened the pines of Dormillière, and the old Church stood majestically forward among them, throwing back its head and keeping sleepless watch towards the opposite side. Gradually receding, too, the Manoir showed less and less gable among its mass of foliage.

If the Church is one great institution of that country, the St. Lawrence is no less another,—displaying thirty miles unbroken blue on a clear day in the direction of the distant hill of Montreal, and on the other hand, towards Lake St. Peter, a vista oceanlike and unhorizoned.   In certain regions numerous flat islands, covered by long grasses and rushes intersected by labyrinthine passages, hide the boatman from the sight of the world and form innumerable nooks of quiet which have a class of scenery and inhabitants altogether their own.   As the chaloupe glides around some unsuspected corner, the crane rises heavily at the splash of a paddle, wild duck fly off low and swiftly, the plover circle away in bright handsome flocks, the gorgeous kingfisher leaves his little tree.   In the water different spots have their special finny denizens.   In one place a broad deep arm of the river—which throws off a dozen such arms, each as large as London's Thames, without the main stream appearing a whit less broad—shelters among its weeds exhaustless tribes of perch and pickerel ; in another place a swifter and profounder current conceals the great sturgeon and lion-like maskinongé; while among certain shallower, less active corners, the bottom is clothed with muddy cat fish.

They approached a region of this kind, skimmed along by spirited athletic strokes, and had arrived at the head of the low-lying archipelago just described, where they came upon a motionless figure sitting fishing in a punt, some distance along a broad passage to the left.

Short blue blouse, little cap and flat-bottomed boat, the appearance of the figure at that hour made one with the drifting mists and rural strangeness of the landscape, and Chrysler knew it was Le Brun, and remarked so to Haviland.

" Without doubt, Bonhomme is part of nature and unmistakable. —Holà Bonhomme ! "

" Mo-o-o-o-nseigneur," he sung in reply, without looking up or taking further notice of them.

Haviland gave a few more vigorous strokes.

" How does it bite, Bonhomme ? "

" A little badly, monseigneur ; all perch here ; one pickerel.   Shall we enter the little channels ? "

" I do not wish to enter the little channels : I remain here."

They were soon fishing beside him, Chamilly at one end of the skiff intent upon his sport.   The old man's flat punt was littered with perch.   How early he must have risen !   He was small of figure, weathered of face, simple and impassive of manner.

" Good day," Chrysler opened ; " the weather is wettish."

" It is morningy, Monsieur."—

" My son knows you, Monsieur," he said again humbly, after a pause.

As Chrysler could not recall his son, as such, he waited before replying.

" He saw you at Benoit's."

Still Chrysler paused.

" On Sunday."

" A—ha, now I remember. That fine young man is your son ?"

" That fine young man, sir," he assented with perfect faith.

After adjusting a line for Chrysler, he continued.

" Do you not think, monsieur, that my son is fine enough for Josephte Benoit ?"

" Assuredly. Does he like her ?"

" They are devoted to each other."

" If she accepts him then, why not ? You do not doubt your son ?"

" Never, Monsieur! what is different is Jean. He thinks my François too poor for his Josephte, and he is for ever planning to discourage their love. Grand Dieu, he is proud! Yet his father and I were good friends when we were both boys. He wants Mlle. Josephte to take the American."

" Reassure yourself; that will never be. No, Bonhomme, trust to me ; that shall never be," exclaimed Chamilly.

" How did you come to know these parties, sir," he put in in English. But without awaiting an answer he continued : " Benoit is crazy to marry his daughter to that rowdy. Benoit was always rather off on the surface, but he has usually been shrewder at bottom. Cuiller infatuates him. He hasn't a single antecedent, but has been treating Benoit so much to liquor and boasting, that the foolish man follows him like a dog."

" My son has been to Montreal,—he has done business," said the Bonhomme with pride—" he is a good young man—and he had plenty of money before he lost it on the journey."

" How did he lose his money ?"

" Some one stole it. He was coming down to marry Josephte. If he had had his money Jean would have let her take him.—But he can earn more."

"There was a mysterious robbery of François' money on the steam boat a couple of weeks ago," said Chamilly in English again, " I shall have to lend him some to set him up in business here, but mustn't do it till after my election."

CHAPTER XXVI.

THE IDEAL STATE.

The air, meanwhile, had been losing its dampness and the mist disappearing, when Haviland drew up his rod and threw it into the boat, and called upon his friend to turn and look at the sunrise.

American sunsets and sunrises, owing to the atmosphere, are famous for their gorgeousness; but some varieties are especially noble. Mountain ones charm by floods of lights and coloring over the heights and ravines, to whose character indeed the sky effects make but a clothing robe, and it is the mountains, or the combination, that speaks. But looking along this glassy avenue of water, flushed with the reflection, it was the great sunrise itself, in its own unobstructed fullness, spreading higher and broader than ever less level country had permitted the Ontarian to behold it, that towered above them over the reedy landscape, in grand suffusions and surges of color.

"It is in Nature," said Chamilly, comprehending that Chrysler felt the scene, "that I can love Canada most, and become renewed into efforts for the good of her human sons. I feel in the presence of this,"—he waved his hand upward, "that I could speak of my ideas."

"You would please me. You said a nation must have a reason for existing and that Canada should have a clear ideal of hers. What is the raison d'être of Canada?"

"*To do pre-eminently well a part of the highest work of all the world! If by being a nation we can advance mankind; if by being a nation we can make a better community for ourselves ; our aims are founded on the highest raison d'être,—the ethical spirit.* We must deliberately mark out our work on this principle; and if we do not work upon it we had better not exist."

Then Haviland related to Chrysler freely and fully the comprehensive plan which he had worked out for the building of the nation.

"First of all," he said, "as to ourselves, there are certain things we must clearly take to mind before we begin :

"That we cannot do good work without making ourselves a good people ;

"That we cannot do the best work without being also a strong and intellectual people ;

"And that we cannot attain to anything of value at haphazard ; but must deliberately choose and train for it."

"Labors worthy of Hercules !" ejaculated the old gentleman.

"Worthy of God," the young one replied. The difference of age between himself and the Ontarian seemed to disappear, and he proceeded confidently :

"The foundation must be the Ideal Physical Man. We must never stop short of working until,—now, do not doubt me, sir,— every Canadian is the strongest and most beautiful man that can be thought. No matter how utterly chimerical this seems to the parlor skeptic who insists on our seeing only the common-place, it cannot be so to the true thinker who knows the promises of science and reflects that a nation can turn its face to endeavours which are impossible for a person. Physical culture must be placed on a more reasonable basis, and made a requisite of all education. We need a Physical Inspector in every School. We need to regularly encourage the sports of the country. We require a military term of training, compulsory on all young men, for its effect in straightening the person and strengthening the will. We must have a nation of stern, strong men—a careless people can never rise ; no deep impression, no fixed resolve, will ever originate from easy-going natures.

"Next, the most crying requirement is True Education. The source of all our political errors and sufferings is an ignorant electorate, who do not know how to measure either the men or the doctrines that come before them. There is necessity in the doctrine of the State's right over secular education. Democracy, gives you and me an inalienable interest, social and political, in the education of each voter, because its very principle is the right to choose our rulers. As to religious education, that of course is sacred, where it does not encroach on the State's right, and the arrangement I favor is that secular studies be enforced during certain hours, and the use of the school buildings granted to religious instructors at others."

" I notice you say true education."

"A man is being truly educated when his training is exactly levelled at what he ought to be :—first of all a high type of man in general, and next, a good performer of his calling. Let him have a scheme of facts that will give him an idea of the ALL : then show him his part in it.

" Let him be taught in a simple way the logic of facts.

" Let him be taught to seek the best sources only of information.

" Let him be taught in school the falsity of the chief political sophisms.

"Let him be branded with a few business principles of life in general : such as how much to save, and where to put it, and the wisdom of insurance.

" Let him learn these three maxims of experience :

"Gain experience.

"Gain experience at the lowest possible price.

" Never risk gaining the same experience twice.

"Seek for him, in fine, not learning so much as wisdom, the essence of learning.

" But especially, let every Canadian be educated to see The National Work, and how to do it.

" In short, educate for what you require and educate most for the greatest things you require, and in manner such that every one may be equipped to stand anywhere without help, and fight a good battle.

" It is an Ideal Character, however, a character perfectly harmonized with his destinies as a soul, and his condition as a citizen, that is the most important armour in the panoply of the Canadian. Purity and elevation of the national character must be held sacred as the snowy peaks of Olympus to the Greek. And as those celestial summits could never have risen to their majesty without foundations of more humble rocks and earth ; so we must lay foundations for our finer aspirations by the acquirement of certain basal habits :

" The Habit of Industry.

" The Habit of Economy.

" The Habit of Progress.

" The Habit of Seriousness.

" In other words the habits of honestly acquiring, keeping and improving, all good things, material, intellectual and moral, and of dealing with the realities of things.

" The Habit of Seriousness may seem strange to insist upon, but one has only to mark the injury to everything noble, of an atmosphere of flippancy and constant strain after smart language. There is nothing in flippancy to have awe of—any one can learn the knack of it—but it is foolish and degrading, while seriousness is the color of truth itself."

" As to the Habit of Industry, there is no other way that can be depended upon for becoming wealthy in goods, or learning, or in good deeds. Materially, if we can learn to employ all our available time at something, we shall be the richest of nations. Why have we so many men idling about the villages? Why do so many women simply live on a relative? How different the country would look if the man spent his waste moments in building a gallery, an oriel window, or an awning, to his house, and the idle girl practised some home manufacture. The prosperity of certain Annapolis valley farmers once struck me. 'Do you know why it is?' said a gentleman who was born there. 'The forefathers of these people were a colony of weavers, *and there is a loom in every house.'*

"The Habit of Economy is simply making the best use of our possessions and powers.

"The Habit of Progress, or of constantly seeking to improve, is to be deeply impressed. It alone will bring us everything. It is never time to say, "Let us remain as we are."

"We could attend to some minor habits with benefit. How the popular intelligence would be improved, for instance, by :—

"A habit of asking for the facts.

"A habit of thinking before asserting.

"A mean between liberality and tenacity of conviction.

"Now one more piece of equipment, but it is the highest: The Canadian, if he is to live a life thoroughly scaled on the scale of the reasonable, must place the greatest importance on those interests which transcend all his others, his future fare beyond this make-shift existence; his relations to the unseen world; and how to lay hold on purity and righteousness. Think what he may of them, he should at any rate think. Let him set apart times to ponder over these matters : and for this, I say that to be a lofty and noble nation, we must all borrow the rational observance of the Sabbath, not as a day merely of rest and still less of flighty recreation, but a necessary period devoted to man's thought upon his more tremendous affairs."

After the equipment of the ideal Canadians, Chamilly proceeded to describe their work. They were to see its pattern above them in the skies—The Perfect Nation.

Among themselves a few great ideas were to be striven for: " We must be One People," " Canada must be Perfectly Independent : " "There must be No Proletariat."

The principle of government was to be "Government by the Best Intelligence."

" We must try to amend unfair distributions of wealth. Yet not to take from the rich, but give to the poor. Fortunes should be looked upon as national, and we should seek means to bring the wealthy to apply their fortunes to patriotic uses. The surroundings of the poor should be made beautiful. No labour should be wasted. Men should learn several occupations, and Government find means of instant communication between those who would work and those who would employ. The lot of the poor must not be made hopeless from generation to generation ! "

The next demand of the Ideal was, " There must be No Vice."

" The difficulties ! " sighed Chrysler.

" We ought to be ashamed to complain till we have done as well as Sweden."

" Again, we must stamp our action with the Spirit of Organization. The nation must work all together as a whole. The public plan must be clearly disseminated, and especially the aim 'To do pre-eminently well our portion of the improvement of the world.' Consecrated by our ideal also we must seek to draw together, and foster a national distinctiveness. Canada must mean to us the Sacred Country, and our young men learn to weigh truly the value of such living against foreign advantages. For there is no surety of any excellence equal to a national atmosphere of it. They have always been artists in Italy ; they have always been sternly free in Scotland : for a word of glory the French rush into the smoke of battle: the Englishman is a success in courage and practicality ; the German has not given his existence in vain to thoroughness ; nor the American to business.   Let us make to ourselves proper customs and peculiarities, like the good old New Year's call, the Winter Carnival, the snow-shoe costume, and a secular procession of St. Jean Baptiste.   Tradition too !   Why should we forget the virtues of our fathers ; or perhaps still better their faults ? Let the man who was a hero—Daulac; Brock; the twelve who sortied at Lacolle Mill ; our deathless three hundred of Chateauguay,—never to be forgotten.   Have them in our books, our school books, our buildings.   Make a Fund for Tablets, so that the people may read every-where : 'Here died McGee, who loved this nation.'   'Papineau spoke here.'   'In this house dwelt Heavysege.'   So might all Canada be a Quebec of memories."

He held that the office of our literature and art was to express the spirit of our work.   "Nor let the poet," he said, "find the keystone of our spirits dull ; let 'him not fear he sings a vain song when he leaves that voice lingering in some vale of ours that conjures about it forever its moment of richest beauty and romance."

In dress, in manners, we should be common-sense, tasteful and fearless, and in the development of our territory energetic and full of hope.   "Believe me, sir, we shall yet learn how to have bright firesides on the shores of the Arctic."

"And where is our world-work ?"   Chrysler asked, like one awakening.

"Wherever there is world-work undone that we can reach to do."

"Think," cried he, finally, "of a country that lives, as I am suggesting, on the deepest and highest principle of the seen and the unseen —what has been the aspiration of the lonely great of other nations, the clear purpose of all is this : what have been the virtues of a few in the past, determined here to be those of the whole ; and every citizen ennobled by the consciousness that he is equally possessed of the common glory ! "

" It can be done ! Heaven and earth tell us that all is under laws of cause and effect, and that this, which has been once, can be made universal. I hear the voice of Science, ' It can be done. It can be done !' I hear the voice of Duty, ' It must be done !' Inextinguishable voices ! ! "

" It comes to me so vividly that I almost point you to that sunrise and say, ' See you beautiful city whose palaces and churches tower with the grace and splendors of all known architecture; those rural plains and vales of park and garden, where every home nestles so as one could not conceive it more lovely ; that race of heroes and goddesses in strength and thought ; those proud tablets and monuments of national and international honor and achievement and blessing.' And if any say, ' How can we attain to that greatness ?' I would write him this amulet : ' Begin at the POSSIBLE ! ' "

The patriot ended, and when he had finished, Chrysler exclaimed :

" Work it out, Haviland ! If a convert is any use to you, take me over and send me forth. It's a noble scheme. But, for Heaven's sake, fortify yourself. How many proselytes do you expect in the first hundred years ? "

" You forget," replied Haviland. " I have always this faithful little legion of Dormillière. Has not Lareau said," and he smiled half in joke, half seriously, " that we are a people of ideals."

They returned to their fishing in silence, broken by a meditative query now and then from Chrysler, but no movement of curiosity from the Bonhomme.

CHAPTER XXVII.

JOSEPHTE.

"Sister Elisâ," lisped Rudolphe, the tiny boy. (In the garden the children of the farmer of the domain, and of Pierre, were playing together.) "Mr. Ch'ysl' has told me he was a Canadian."

"Did he say so, *mon fin?*" asked motherly ten-year-old Elisâ, picking a "belle p'tite" flower for the little fellow, whom she held by the hand.

"He's not Canadian," put in the large boy, Henri, with contempt befitting his twelve years of experience. "Because he doesn't speak French. He's an English."

"Speaking French don't make a Canadian," answered Elisâ. "The Honorable says every one who is native in Canada is a Canadian, speak he French, speak he English."

"O, well—the Honorable — the Honorable —" retorted Henri, testily.

While this went on, the voice of Josephte could be heard singing low and happy, in a corner of the walk of pines which surrounded the garden and the back of the grounds :

> "Eglantine est la fleur que j'aime
> La violette est ma couleur...." *

Next, lower, but as if stirred softly by the lingering strain rather than feeling its sadness :

---

* "Eglantine is the flower I love,
My color is the violet."

" .... Dans le souci tu vois l'emblème
Des chagrins de mon triste cœur." *

When she got thus far, she stopped and called out, cheerfully :—
" Come along, my little ones ; come along ; come along and recite
your duties ! "   And in a trice they all raced in and were panting in
a row about her.

Thus one sultry afternoon, Mr. Chrysler found her sitting, book
and sewing on her lap and only a rosary about her neck to relieve the
modest black dress, whose folds,

" Plain in their neatness,"

accorded well with her indefinably gentle bearing.   Seeing him, she
stopped and dropped her head, like a good convent maiden.

" Procedez, ma'amselle," he said, nodding benevolently.   " Do
not disturb yourself."

" But, monsieur," she said, and blushed in confusion.

" Go on.   I shall be interested in these young people's lessons."

" As monsieur wishes," she replied.   " Now, my little ones, your
catechism."

They ranged themselves in a line.

" Elisâ, thee first ; repeat the Commandments of God."

Elisâ commenced a rhyming paraphrase of the Ten Commandments.

" Ah, no, cherie,—more reverence.   Say it as to the Holy Virgin."

Elisâ went through it in a soft manner to the end.

" Rudolphe ; the Seven Commandments of the Church."

The childish accents of the little one repeated them :—

> 1. Mass on Sundays thou shalt hear
>   And on feasts commanded thee.
>
> 2. Once at least in every year,
>   Must thy sins confessed be.

* " ....The symbol shall the emblem prove
Of my sad heart and eyelids wet."

3. Thy Creator take at least
   At Easter with humility..

4. And keep holy every feast,
   Whereof thou shalt have decree.

5. Quatre-temps, Vigils, fasts are met,
   And in Lent entirely.

6. Fridays flesh thou shalt not eat ;
   Saturdays the same shall be.

7. Church's every tithe and fee
   Thou shalt pay her faithfully."

"Henri, what is the Church which Jesus Christ has established ?"

"The Church which Jesus Christ has established," said he stoutly, "is the Church Catholic, Apostolic and Roman."

The next was Henri's eight year old sister.

"Can anyone be saved outside of the Church Catholic, Apostolic and Roman ?"

"No," (solemnly,) "out of the Church there is no salvation."

"Say now the Act of Faith all together."

"My God," said the children in unison, "I believe firmly all that the Holy Catholic Church believes and teaches, because it is you who have said it and you are Truth Itself."

"You may rest yourselves."

"Chrysler was most curious regarding what he heard thus instilled. The thought struck him: "There's something like that in our Calvinism too."

"My dear demoiselle," he said aloud, "as I am a Protestant—"

"A Protestant, sir !" She regarded him with visibly extraordinary emotions, and involuntarily crossed herself.

"It is impossible !"

It was the first time a Protestant and she had ever been face to face. "Monsieur," she appealed in agitation "why do you not enter the bosom of the true Church ?"

"Must one not act as he believes ?"

"But, sir," said the dear girl, painfully, still regarding him with great wonder, "on studying true doctrine, the saints will make you believe ; the priest can baptize you. He will be delighted, I am certain, to save a soul from destruction." She could not restrain the flow of a tear.

"My child," Chrysler said, for he saw that curiosity had led him too far : "Leave this to God, who is greater than you or I and knows every heart."

"Monsieur, then, believes in God !" Her present astonishment was equal to that before.

The rising voices of the children relieved him. That of Elisâ, who sat in a ring of the rest, nodding her head decidedly and rhythmically, was conspicuous :

"I am going to join the Sisterhood of the Holy Rosary and go to church early, early, often, often, four times a day, and pray, pray, and say my paters and my aves, and gain my indulgences, and be more devout than Sister Jesus of God ; and then I am going to take the novitiate and wear a beautiful white veil and fast every day, and at last—at last—I am going to be a Religieuse."

"What name will you take, Elisâ ?"

"I have decided," the little convent girl responded, "to take the name of ' Sister St. Joseph of the Cradle.' "

"Mais, that is pretty, that ! But I prefer ' St. Mary of the Saviour.' "

"What are you going to be ?" Elisâ asked of the smaller girl.

"I will be—I will be—I will take my first communion."

"I have taken it already," replied Elisâ, with superiority.

"Henri ! Henri ! it is your turn."

" I am going to be an advocate."

" And I am going to be a Rouge," replied little Rudolphe.

" Hah,—we are all Rouges," replied Henri.

" O, well—I will be, then—Monseigneur, like Monsieur Chamilly."

The garden stretched behind the manor-house. Along its paths these children delighted to explore the motherly currant-bushes. Old-fashioned flowers stocked it, and, as Chrysler walked away among them, they reminded him of the simple gardens of his childhood before the showy house-plant era had modernized our grounds. There were erect groups and rows of hollyhocks; monkshood offered its clusters of blue caps; striped tulips and crimson poppies flourished in beds of generous shapes; delicate astors, rich dahlias, and neat little bachelors' buttons peeped in crowds from green freshnesses. This was one of Madame's domains, where she walked, weeded and superintended every morning in broad straw hat and apron; and it was to Chrysler one of the attractions of the Manoir.

CHAPTER XXVIII.

GRANDMOULIN.

" Que Demosthènes,
En haranguant,
Entraine Athènes,
Come un torrent !"....
—JACQUES VIGER—LE JARGON DU BEL-ESPRIT.

The events to which all others were leading now began to happen.

The great nomination day,—Sunday—is here. Mass is over, the whole parish, aye and crowds from far and and near behind, surge all over the square, where the Church looks down upon them in serenity and silence.

When Chrysler came up, the Cure and his vicar were sitting on their gallery, and a man of strong frame stood upon the crier's rostrum looking round with the assertive consciousness that he was a recognized figure. His face wore a beard of strong but thin black wisps, which would have been Vandyke in form had it been heavier, but allowed the forcible outlines of his chin and cheek to be visible ; and his locks, imitated by many a follower throughout the Province, were worn like Gambetta's in a long and swelling black mass behind. His countenance, evidently from long experience, was so controlled that no trace of natural expression could be discerned upon it beyond an appearance of caution and diplomacy ; but whatever its specific character, it bore without gainsay the stamp of power.

The man was Grandmoulin.

After looking this way and that way for several moments allowing the assemblage to hush, he began in a quiet tone.

" My friends ! "

He paused deliberately some moments to permit the people's curiosity to concentrate upon him.

" My brothers ! "

This with a rising, powerful voice.—Then higher :

" French—Canadians ! ! " separating the two words.

The audience strained with attention to hear him. What he had to say next became a matter of suspense.

Then with inflection of passionate enthusiasm :

" Canadian FRENCHMEN ! ! ! " he cried, hurling out all his force. And the people could no longer restrain themselves ; the rhetorical artifice took them by storm, and they shouted and cheered with one loud, far-echoing, unanimous voice.

Grandmoulin kept his attitude erect and immovable.

" My friends," he proceeded, when the applause began to subside, " I address you as heritors and representatives of a glorious national title. To wear it—to be called ' Frenchman ' is to stand in the ranks of the nobility of the human race. I address you as a generous, a great, a devoted people, a people brave of heart and unequalled in intellectual ability, a people proud of themselves, their deeds and the deeds of their fathers in New France and in the fair France of the past, a people above all intensely national, patriotic, jealous for the advancement of their tongue and their race. I address you as faithful of the ancient Church which was founded on the Petrine Rock, and names itself Catholic, Apostolic, Roman ; whose altars God has preserved unshaken through the centuries amid terrible hosts of enemies, bitter oppressions, diabolical persecutions ; of whose faith your hearts, your bodies, your race itself, are the consecrated depositories set apart and blessed of Heaven."

" I address you further, Frenchmen of Canada, as an oppressed remnant, long crushed and evil treated under alien conquerors ; who despoiled you of your dominion, your freedom and your future, and whose military despotism, history records, spurned your cry during eighty years with unspeakable arrogance ; till you rose like men in the despair of the '37, for the simplest rights, brandishing in your hands poor scythes and knives against armies with cannon, O my compatriots !—and compelled them to dole you a little justice !

" The brave and generous who still remain of the generation before, recount to you those living scenes, and your hearts take part with the wronged and valiant of your blood !

" In this secluded countryside you see too little how they still insult you. Ask yourselves frankly whether that for which our nation strove has ever yet been had. What have we gained ? Is not the battle still to be fought ? There are no facts more patent than that the English are our conquerors, that they rule our country, that they are aliens, heretics, enemies of our Holy Religion, and that they are heaping up unrighteous riches, while we are becoming despised and poor.

" Think not that I speak without emotions in my breast. There was a day, my poor French-Canadian brothers,—a solemn day, when I bound myself by a great oath to the cause of my people. It was when my father told me, his voice choking with tears, of the murder of my grandfather, ignominiously thrown from the gallows for the felony of patriotism ! Was I wrong to rise in grief and wrath, and swear with tears and prayers before our good Ste. Anne that I would never rest or taste a pleasure until I free the French-Canadians ?"

" ' It is I who will defend my race and my religion ! ' cried I then, and I have ever striven to do this, and still so strive."

Having thus played along each different key of his hearer's prejudices, he turned them towards his end.

I

" It is possible you may think I have been speaking of everything but politics, and that you are asking yourselves what I really mean. Do you know what this election signifies ? *It is a contest of the French with the English.* It is a question whether that arrogant minority shall continue to impose their ideas, their leaders, their execrable heresies, their taxes and restrictions upon this great French-Canadian Province—the only country which you have been able to hold for your own. You are here, at least, the majority ! If their artifices have succeeded in excluding you from a part in governing the Dominion, there is one thing left ; *you can govern this Province if you stand by me !* If you stand by my me you can make our country purely and powerfully French ! The ballot gives us the government : we will legislate the English. We will repay their oppressions with taxes and leave the Frenchman free ; we will overvalue their properties, and undervalue our own ; we will divide their constituencies ; we will proclaim parishes out of townships ; we will deprive them of offices, harass their commerce, vex their heretical altars ; we will force new privileges from the Federal power ; we will colonize the public lands with our own people exclusively, and repatriate our children lost ; we will possess ourselves of those palaces and that vast wealth they wring from our labor, and finally, free as these great stretches of the valley, we shall live at peace in our own land."

A sullen murmur passed about. The passions were being roused. " The English eat the French-Canadians," repeated several.

" Messieurs of Dormillière, you can judge of me ! They have said of me all sorts of calumnies, all kinds of insinuations. I have been painted as black as the evil spirits. Men are here who will tell you 'Grandmoulin is a hypocrite ; Grandmoulin is a robber, a liar, a libertine,'—that I have ruined my Province and sold my people and committed all the list of mortal sins. But, my brothers, I turn from those who assert these wicked falsehoods and I justify myself to you.

" Because I have not sought peace with the strong—because I have not acted a vanquished to the victors—because I have suffered—but that is nothing—because I have freely poured out every energy, as I do to-day," (and there was certainly vast physical effort in the output he was then making of himself) "they have branded me that disturber, that robber, that murderer, that liar and that villain.

" Messieurs, let me tell you a secret that will explain ! Scan close and you will find that there is no man who says these things of me who is not either a friend of the English, and traitor to you, or else has been rejected by my associates as unworthy to represent our patriotic ambitions. I must speak even of the agreeable young man of intellect and eloquence who opposes me. I do not blame him : I forgive him. He is young and inexperienced, and he sees things from certain aspects only. Have you never considered that it was natural for one whose father was an Englishman, and whose Protestant grandfather came across the seas among the army that conquered us, to look from a standpoint different from ours. If his birth and sympathies lead him in another direction from me, and my enemies have succeeded in prejudicing his mind, make allowance for him as I myself do, *and trust me.* I adjure you by the holy names of Mary and Joseph, I am your friend : understand only that Grandmoulin is your friend ! Let the confidence be complete, and the triumph of your race in the Province of Quebec is secure !"

To Chrysler's utter surprise, the orator, pausing a moment, singled him out; pointed his finger towards him, and, turning to the people. cried : " Have I not said Mr. Haviland was a friend of your conquerors ? Let me show you his adviser at this crisis of his plans !"

Grandmoulin knew he was in a community saturated with the Rouge tradition. He knew that even with all the weak and corruptible elements of the " back parishes " his chances were inferior on their face to Chamilly's, and he felt that he must at least retain his adherents here or lose the county.   It was only after a final, truly magnificent effort of eloquence that he withdrew, and cheers upon cheers followed him, especially from a party among whom Cuiller, in a state of intoxication, was prominent.   It was the first time that Grandmoulin had appeared in the neighborhood, and he had evidently created a great impression.

CHAPTER XXIX.

CHAMILLY.

" Mais, n'avons-nous pas, je vous prie,
  Encore de plus puissants liens ?
A tout preferons la patrie :
  Avant tout soyons Canadiens."

               —POPULAR SONG.

Chamilly rose upon the rostrum when Grandmoulin went down. He opened quietly, after the exciting peroration of his opponent, and in a manner which lulled and calmed the assembly.

"People of Dormillière, I have had a cause for wonder during Mr. Grandmoulin's discourse. I have been wondering at the perfect courage with which he invents a fact, a reason, a principle, an emotion, in cases where almost the whole world knows that none of these exist.

"I am accounted a person informed in the events of '37. I have studied all the accounts and documents that are accessible, and have made a point of conversing with the survivors of that time. I state with the fullest knowledge, and you have long known the value of my word, that it is a falsehood that Mr. Grandmoulin's grandfather died a martyr as he has alleged, nor is he known to have been concerned in the rebellion in any way."

This statement created a visible sensation over the audience.

"Zotique called out : 'The National Liar !'"

Grandmoulin remained immovable.

"His assertion that I am an Englishman," went on Chamilly, "is as absurd as it is futile here. Friends of mine through my youth, and children of the friends of my forefathers, whose lives arose and declined in this place like ours, am I not bound to you by ties which forbid that I should be named a stranger!"

(Cries of "Oui, Oui," "Nôtre frère!" and "Nôtre Chamilly!")

"Mr. Grandmoulin speaks a falsehood of perhaps not less importance in his assertion that the English are oppressing us. Where is the oppression of which he makes cry? The very existence of each of you in his full liberty and speaking French ought to be a sufficient argument. Speak, act, worship, buy, sell,—who hinders us so long as we obey the laws? Would you like a stronger evidence of our freedom? Grandmoulin himself presents it when he proclaims his violent incitations! Of oppression by our good fellow-citizens, let then no more be said.—

"The object of Mr. Grandmoulin in these bold falsifications is I think sufficiently suspected by you, when you have it on the evidence of your senses that they are invented. Let us leave both them and him aside and keep ourselves free to examine that theme of far transcending importance, *the true position of the French-Canadians*.

"What is our true position? Is it to be a people of Ishmaelites, who see in every stranger an enemy, who, having rejected good-will, shall have chosen to be those whose existence is an intrigue—a people accepting no ideas, and receiving no benefits? Will they be happy in their hatred? Will they progress? Will they be permitted to exist?

"Or shall their ideas be different? Tell me, ye who are of them; is it more natural or not that they shall open their generous hearts to everyone who will be their friend, their minds to every idea, their conceptions to the noon-day conception of the fraternity of mankind, liberty, equality, good-will? Is it more natural or not that we should find pride in a country and a nation which have accepted our name and history, and are constantly seeking our citizen-like affection to make the union with us complete? French-Canadians, the honor of this Dominion, which promises to be one of the greatest nations of the earth, is peculiarly yours. You are of the race which were the first to call themselves Canadians! The interests of your children are bound up in its being; your honor in its conduct; your glory in its success. Work for it, think on it, pray for it; let no illusion render you untrue to it: beware of the enemy who would demolish the foundation of one patriotism under pretext of laying the stones of another."

"Canadians!"—He lingered on the sound with tones of striking richness which sank into the hearts of his hearers. "Canadians! —Great title of the future, syllable of music, who is it that shall hear it in these plains in centuries to come, and shall forget the race who chose it, and gave it to the hundred peoples who arrive to blend in our land? To *your* stock the historic part and the gesture of respect is assigned, from the companies of the incoming stream. My brothers, let us be benign, and accept our place of honor. Identify yourselves with a nation vaster than your race, and cultivate your talents to put you at its head."

He said he had no condemnation, however, for those who were rightly proud of the deeds of the French race and its old heroes.

"I have nothing but the enthusiasm of a comrade for any true to the noble feelings which it would be a shame to let die! I entreat that they be cherished, and let them incite us to new assurance of our capabilities for enterprises fitting to our age. Let the virtues of old take new forms, and courage will still be courage, hospitality hospitality, and patriotism patriotism! Away with dragging for inglorious purposes the banner of the past through the dust of the present! Let the present be made glorious, and not inglorious, in its own kind, and the past shine on at its enchanted distance of beauty!"

        *   *   *   *

"What shall that greatness be—that splendor of our Canada to come ?" He pictured its possibilities in grand vistas. The people were spell-bound by noble hopes and emotions which carried them upward. Involuntarily, as Chrysler looked at his face and bearing, he was reminded of the prophets, and the old white church behind seemed to be rising and throwing back its head, and with-drawing its thoughts into some proud region of the great and super-natural. The old man forgot the crowd and the crowd totally forgot Chrysler :

" Canadians !" Chamilly closed, his figure drawn up like a hero's and his rich voice sounding the name again with that wonderful utterance, "the memories of our race are compatible only with the good of the world and our country. If you are unwilling to accept me on this basis, do not elect me, for I will only express my convictions."

CHAPTER XXX.

AN ORATION UNDER DIFFICULTIES.

"On high in yonder old church tower,
* * * * * * *
The ancient bell rings out the hour,
Sometimes with voice of wondrous power."

—JOHN BREAKENRIDGE.

Monsieur Editor Quinet mounted the platform and stood there, cool and masterful.

At the same moment the Curé in his black gown, bolted up from his chair beside his young vicar, on the gallery of the parsonage, and regarding the orator with indignation, raised his breviary towards the church with outstretched arm.

" Messieurs, what ruins us " . . . . Quinet commenced.

His sentence was shattered to pieces !

" KLING-KLANG-G-G-G ! " a loud church bell resounded from one of the towers, sending a visible shock over the assembly and drowning the succeeding words.

" What ruins us " . . . . Quinet, with imperturbable composure, commenced again in a louder voice.

A crashing peal from the opposite belfry replied to the first and compelled him to stop.

The Curé, swelling with triumph, marched up and down his gallery, turning quickly at each end ; while the bells of both the towers, swinging confusedly in their belfries, sent forth one horrible continued torrent of clangor over the amazed crowd.

The speaker was soon convinced that no amount of cool waiting would prevail. He did, therefore, what was a more keenly effective continuation of his sentence than any words,—raised his finger and pointed it steadily for a few moments at the Curé, and then withdrew.

For many a day the story of Quinet and the bells was told in Dormillière.

CHAPTER XXXI.

LIBERGENT.

During the addresses, Libergent, Chamilly's nominal opponent, seemed to do nothing more than stand behind the rostrum and let things proceed. Libergent, lawyer, was a man of a shrewd low order of ability. About forty years of age and medium height, his compact, athletic physique, partly bald head, small but well rounded skull, close iron-grey hair and moustache would have made him a perfect type of the French military man, were it not for a sort of stoop of determination, which, however, added.to his appearance of athletic alertness, while it took away much dignity. The expression of his face was not bad. The decided droop of the corners of the mouth, and hardness of his grey-brown eyes indicated, it is true, a measure of irritability, but on the whole, the objectionable element of the expression was only that of a man who was accustomed to measure all things on the scale of commonplace personal advantage. His life was not belied by his appearance. He found his chief pleasures in fishing, and shooting, and kept a trotter of rapid pace. His quarters were comfortable in the sense of the smoker and sportsman. When he did not wear an easier costume for convenience, his shining hat and broad-cloth coat would have been the envy of many a city confrère. He lived a very moderate, regular life : now and then took a little liquor with a friend, but always with some sage remark against excess ; made himself for the most part a reasonable and sufficiently agreeable companion; and had no higher tastes, unless a collection of coins, well mounted and arranged and at times added to, may claim that title.   He therefore considered Haviland stark mad in spending so much money and brains upon nonsense; and the subject made him testy when he reviewed his refusal to accept some arrangement by which they could share the local political advantages between them.

"Politics is a sphere of business like any other," he said.   "Haviland is doing the injury to himself and me that a theorist in business always does.   He makes himself a cursed nuisance."

CHAPTER XXXII.

MISÉRICORDE.

Fiercely the election stirred the energies of Dormillière. For more than a generation, enthusiasm for political contest had been a local characteristic; but now the feelings of the village,—as pronounced and hereditary a "Red" stronghold, as Vincennes across the river was hereditarily "Blue,"—may be likened only to the feeling of the Trojans at the famous siege of Troy. Their Seigneur was the Hector, and their strand beheld debarking against it the boldest pirates of the French-Canadian Hellas.

In Chrysler's walks he met signs of the excitement even where a long stroll brought him far back into the country.

The one of such corners named Miséricorde from its wretchedness, was a hamlet of thirty or forty cabins crowded together among some scrub trees in the midst of a stony moor. The inhabitants, of whom a good share were broken-down beggars and nondescript fishermen, varied their discouraged existences by drinking, wood sawing and doing odd jobs for the surrounding farmers, while their slatternly women idled at the doors and the children grew up wild, trooping over the surrounding waste. Politically, the place was noted for its unreliability. It was well known that every suffrage in it was open to corruption. In ordinary times the Rouges troubled themselves little about this, but the strong combination they had now to fight might make the vote of La Miséricorde of considerable importance; hence, there was some value in the trust which had been placed, at the meeting, in Benoit and Spoon.

Here the latter, even more than at Dormillière, was in his element.

A drinking house, misnamed "hôtel," was the most prominent building in Miséricorde. It would not have ornamented a more respectable locality but, on the whole, possessed a certain picturesqueness among these hovels, and arrested the Ontarian's steps. Stained a dark grey by at least fifty years of exposure, yet slightly tinted with the traces of a by-gone coat of green, it lifted a high peaked roof in air, which in descent, suddenly curving, was carried far out over a high-set front gallery reached by very steep steps. On the stuck-out sign, which was in the same faded condition as the rest of the building, were with difficulty to be distinguished in a suggestion of yellow color the shapes of a large and small French loaf, and the inscription "BOULONGÉ," but the baking had apparently passed away with the paint. While he was curiously surveying this antique bit, a loud voice sounded through the open door, and the heavy form of the "Yankee from Longueuil" precipitated itself proudly, though a trifle unsteadily, forward down the steps and along the middle of the street, swearing, boasting and heading a swarm of men and boys, and loudly drawling a line of Connecticut notions in blasphemy.

It could be seen that Spoon was some kind of a hero in the eyes of Miséricorde. Rich,—for he had paid the drinks; travelled,—they had his assertion for it; courageous,—he could anathematize the Archbishop; Miséricorde had seldom such a novelty all to itself.

"Sacré! To blazes wit' you; set 'em up all roun', you blas' Canaydjin nigger! Du gin, vite donc! John Collins' pour le crowd! I'm a white man, j'sht un homme blanc, j'sht Americain; I'm from the Unyted States, I am! Sacré bleu! Health to all!"

"Health, monsieur!"

"Health, monsieur!"

"A thousand thanks."

"Set 'em up again, baptème, you blas' Canayjin nigger!"

"What does he say!" inquired the landlord, on the verge of being offended.

"Shut up, Potdevin!" said the only man who understood English, fearful lest the second treat should go astray.

"Take!" cried Spoon, in a fit of reconciliation, throwing down a five dollar bill; and at the sight of the money, Potdevin, true landlord, proceeded with the pouring out of the beverages into very small glasses with very thick bottoms.

It was funny, when he had precipitated himself from the door, as above said, to contemplate the fellow with his low hat on one side and far down on his nose, his swelling shirt-front, striped breeches, and mighty brass chain, leading the trooping crowd like some travelling juggler.

All this, however, was election work.

Was it the kind of method Chamilly would approve? There was a short and certain answer.

Which then of Haviland's friends supplied Spoon with money for these only too obvious processes of vote-obtaining. It was not the Honorable, it was not De La Lande, it would not be penurious Benoit?

"Ah, well," Chrysler thought, "I am here but to observe. Am I not under obligations to Zotique, if it be he, which prevent my interfering?"

Another of Chrysler's theories too was exploded. He had long revolved a suspicion that it was Cuiller who had stolen Francois' $750. "Where else, thought he, "does he get these liberal sums to spend?" Once he had ventured to ask Spoon himself about Le Brun's loss but was plumply faced with the growl, "Do you suppose *I* stole it?" and, ashamed of himself, withdrew the theory almost from his own mind. Now he could explain even the American's expenditure.

CHAPTER XXXIII.

BLEUS.

The Haviland party were not the only people alive to the necessities of the contest. It was not seldom that in the Ontarian's walks during those few days, the steady, inscrutable bust of Grandmoulin passed him, driven in one direction or another by Libergent; and sometimes Picault accompanied.

Grandmoulin, indeed, made herculean efforts. His grand *chefs d'œuvre* of oratory—soul stirring appeals, in the name of all that was sacred in honor and religion, for his hypocritical and corrupt purposes, were lifted in noble structures of eloquence before the people, till it seemed as if the lavishness of his genius and labor could only be explained by the desire of challenging the other great orator of the race. The young energies of Haviland responded readily. Their speeches were reported in full for the journals of the cities and watched for everywhere. It was the battle of Cataline and Cicero.

The back parishes were not so soundly " Red " as Dormillière : they usually polled a considerable Blue vote, and were very unstable. Here were concentrated the efforts of Grandmoulin to cajole and Picault to buy.

Once thus Chrysler met Libergent driving Grandmoulin in a "buckboard," while another person sat in the back seat.

"Chrysler! Chrysler!—Listen!" exclaimed the person in the back seat.

Chrysler recognized an Ottawa acquaintance.

" De Bleury ! how do you do ! "

De Bleury put his hand on the reins to stop the vehicle :

" Come up here, Chrysler, we go past the Manoir."

" Thank you, I enjoy walking."

" Come along, come along ; we don't hear excuses in the country. Come, Chrysler, the road is long."

In order not to offend, Chrysler, in spite of his objection to the company, took the unoccupied place behind Grandmoulin.

With Libergent, Chrysler did not reap much in conversation. He was conciliatory in his solitary-like way, and had indulged for once in too much liquor.

" Right Hon'ble Premier,—Sec' State.—Hon'ble Mr. Grandm'lin— all my fren's. You know dose gen'lmen ? All my fren's. Da's all. My fren's goin' make it all right, eh ? I re'spect'ble 'nough." The half-seas-confidential style.

Grandmoulin acknowledged the stranger but gravely, and was at once immutable—oppressed with thought for the country's welfare ! As he sat before Chrysler, and the latter felt the nearness of his broad shoulders and coarse black mass of hair, he could not but picture the man within sinking into littleness and self-contempt at the debased uses of his great talent.

CHAPTER XXXIV.

THE FREEMASON.

Ross de Bleury, the hospitable passenger, was a character. A man of immense physical strength and abounding spirits, soundly and stoutly built, of medium height, brown hair, full eyes and large nostrils, and strong merry lips, always devising some inge-, nious adventure.

One of his schemes, a quarter joke, three-quarters half-serious, was to band together all persons in the Dominion bearing the Ross name into one Canadian clan, he to be chief! His own surname had first of all been simply Bleury, but energetic genealogical researches having discovered to him that the founder of his line in France was a Scotch adventurer, he made bold to resurrect the original name, and add to it what was already a "Charles Réné Marie-Auguste-Raoul-St. Cyr-de Bleury."

Jest, quip and lively saying shortened his route to the doorway of the Circuit Court, and he insisted on Chrysler's passing to his quarters upstairs. The court-room was stocked with dusty benches and tables, on and about which a small but noisy company were postured. One reckless fellow swinging an ale-mug was singing :—

"Tant qu' on le pourra, larirette,
On se damnera, larirà !"

Two girls stood together near the door laughing brazen giggles.

They were the Jalberts, daughters of the innkeeper, who himself with two young politicians from Montreal were impressing on a *habitant:* "If you don't vote for Libergent, you can't go to heaven;" Jalbert being an adherent of the Blues in the hope of "running" Dormillière, if they succeeded, for his license had been taken away by the new movement. The bailiff, a wolfish-looking creature, who was always to be had for drink, also sat there trailing his vast loose moustache over a table. When Grandmoulin entered, a little crowd, like the tail of a comet, followed him into the room. As he passed through he said no word, but drew his cloak about him and moved forward sphinx-like to the bar of the court, where he sat down and commenced to converse with Libergent.

Chrysler mounted the stairs with his entertainer and came upon an entirely different scene. De Bleury's spacious attic was appropriated to the rough and ready convenience of himself alone, and there was something quizzical about its expanses of brown dimnesses and darknesses, the cobwebby light that struggled in through the one high dormer window, the closet-like partition in the middle with a ticket-selling orifice, and the three or four rough chairs, which, with table, newspaper, and a basket of bottles, formed the furniture of this apartment. What work was done here, and how any one could choose such a spot to do work in were questions asked you mysteriously by every object about. As soon as he had waved Chrysler to one of the chairs and sank back upon another into a shadow, he stretched out his hand and pulled the basket of bottles towards him.

"Now, sir, the question of fortune to every good man as he enters the world: 'What will you have.' I don't believe in fate: I believe in fortune: good things for everybody; let him choose. It's the man who won't accept good mouthfuls who is miserable. My Lord, what will you have?"

"I never take anything, thank you!"

"Eh, Mon Dieu! You would'nt have me drink alone! You grieve my soul, Chrysler! *Bois, donc,* my dear friend, we will be merry

together. In this cursed country, among these oxen of the farms, we
don't often meet a civilized friend." In saying this, he was dexter-
ously pulling the cork from a bottle of champagne, which his right
hand now poured into two wine glasses, as skilfully as his left had
whisked them out of a corner of the basket.

"Drink quickly,—Eh bien, you do not wish to? Your health then!
—May you long survive your principles, and experience a blessed
death of gout!"

He quaffed off the glass and poured out another, laughing and
chatting on with such bounding, irresistible spirits that his guest
caught a kind of sympathetic infection. Glass after glass interminable
disappeared down his throat in a kind of intermittent cascade. The
Ontarian laughed more than he had done for many a year.

"But, De Bleury," he got breath to say, "what is your important
capacity here, that they give you such sumptuous quarters?"

"Commercial traveller in the only commerce of the country. We
have no business here, you know, except statesmanship, the trade
in voters, *le métier de ministre.* You see a man;—tell me how much
he owns :—I can tell you his election price. The schedule is simply :
How much taxes does he pay?—Pay my taxes; I vote your side.
There lies the only shame of my Scotch blood that they have
never devised a commerce so obvious. It's like a bailiff we used
to tease; he had no money, poor devil, so when he came into the bar
he used to say to us, 'Make me drunk and have some fun with me.'
'Pay my taxes and have some fun with me :' the same thing, you
see. All men are merchandise. Ross de Bleury alone has no price—
but for a regular good guzzler, I could embezzle a Returning Officer."

A rap sounded on the door of the stairs.

"I resemble my ancestor, the Chevalier Jean Ross, who, when he
was storming a castle in Flanders, exclaimed : "Victory, companions!
we command the door of the wine cellar!"

The words of a Persian proverb :· "You are a liar, but you delight me," passed through Chrysler's mind.

The rap sounded again, and louder, on the door below.

De Bleury's manner changed. He looked at his companion as if revolving some plan; then moving rapidly to the ticket-office-like-closet, he opened a door, and beckoned him in, signing to sit down and keep quiet. The closet was darker than the darkest part of the surrounding garret, for the dormer window in it, similar to the one near the table, was boarded up, all but a single irregular aperture, admitting light enough only to reveal the surroundings after lapse of some time.

De Bleury, however, by holding his purse up to the chink of light, managed to assure himself of the denomination of a bank-note, and then, turning hastily, lifted the sliding door of the ticket-hole a trifle and pushing out the money, left it partly under the slide, letting in a grey beam on their darkness. He then silently applied his eye to an augur-hole above the slide, and waited. Meantime the knock sounded once more and pair of heavy steps came up the stairs, and tramped towards them ; and some indefinable recognition of the heavy tread came vaguely to Chrysler. The steps stopped, the note was withdrawn, the tread sank away down the stairs, and De Bleury, rollicking with suppressed laughter, opened the door.

" You have overseen a ceremony of the Freemasons," he said. "Truly. You don't believe it? I am a Freemason, I *am*, Chrysler," he said, sententiously, with a trace of the champagne, " I have observed a square and compass among the charms at your watch-chain. You know, therefore, your duties towards a brother, not, perhaps, not to see ; but having seen, not to divulge. You understand ?"

" Perfectly, my dear De Bleury. Excuse me, I have an engagement at the Manoir."

K

CHAPTER XXXV.

THE COURSE OF TRUE LOVE.

" Prôneurs de l'ancien régime, dites-moi ce que vous faites de ces belles et riches natures de femmes, qui sortent du sang genereux du peuple ?"

—ETIENNE PARENT.

During the excitement and bustle, Mr. Chrysler also sometimes fell into the modest society of Josephte. The girl seemed sad at these times, and to be losing the serene peace which at first seemed her characteristic. He remarked this to Madame Bois-Hébert one day as he met her sitting in the shades of the pine-walk reading a devotional work.

Madame was a figure still able to command as well as to attract respect. Dignity and ability had not yet departed from her face and bearing, and quietude was the only effect of age upon her, beyond falling cheeks and increasing absorption in exercises of religion.

" Does it not appear to you that your demoiselle is sad ?" he asked.

" It is true, monsieur; her mind is troubled at present."

" The cause is some cavalier."

" You judge correctly. Benoit does not wish her to marry as she desires. And though he wishes her to unite herself to a brute compared with her cavalier, yet the latter is himself an individual of no consequence, and she has been well advised to relinquish him.

" Who is it advises that ?"

" Her friends, who see in her a more lovely destiny. The dear child will make perhaps a Saint. You do not know the expiations and indulgences she has earned these several years by prayers and devotions, her pure nature, her admirable conduct. She is not for the world, but for God."

" What did Josephte herself think ?"

That which Madame had said of her nature was correct enough. She was a delight to the sisters in their sad, austere lives. " She is like an angel, and has the movements of one," they said. Very unlike to, for instance, the daughters Jalbert, those bold and idle girls, whose steady occupation was tom-boying scandalously with chance young men, and jeering impudent jeers at everybody.

Her haunts were in removed and shady nooks, such as the little dell behind the log cabin of the Le Bruns. There, one hot afternoon he found her sitting under the shade of the windmill, dressed as usual in neat black, and as usual lately, pale. The little ones ran, sat and played around her; Henri, Rudolphe and Elisâ in the pride of their enterprise tugging the long beam by which horse or man in the preceding century had turned the conical cap of the mill; their efforts cracking and shaking the crazy roof, but availing nothing except to disturb a crow or two near by, among the white birches through whose clusters gleamed the River in the sun.

What brought Josephte to the Le Brun dell ?

Et quoi ! She was weeping.

Those little children saw not her silent tears. Chrysler beheld them—crystalline drops on pale, soft cheek, emblems of pure heart and secret sorrow; but she checked them when he drew near and sat up composed.

" Mademoiselle," he said, " What is it troubles thee so profoundly ? Tell me ; I am an old man and thy friend."

" Monsieur, Monsieur, I ask your pardon, —she broke again into

tears. Fortunately, all the children were running off among the trees.
—" My sin is great : "

" And what is the offence, my child ? "

Josephte was silent, and the blood rushed over her face.

" I mean thee no ill, Mlle. Josephte. Perhaps I can assist or
advise thee."

" They have promised me to the good God : alas ! and my heart
thinks of a mortal. I never could be like the others.—I cannot
forget," and she broke completely down, sobbing again and again. In
a little while he spoke, hoping to soothe her.

" This may be no more than natural, my dear."

" The natural heart, monsieur, is full of sin ; and that is ten
times worse for a woman. O if I could love God alone ! " and
again she sobbed convulsively.

Trained as the highest type of Catholic mind, her imagination
habitually pictured two worlds—the one of exquisite spiritual light
and purity, and spotless with the presence of saints, of the Virgin ;
of God the Father : the other the world of mankind,—the " world,"
shadowed with wickedness and mourning, and whose pleasure is itself
a sin. She yearned towards the first ; she sank back with acute
sensitiveness from the second. For her, to enter a church was to be
overpowered with the communion of spirits ; to think a single
thought leading away from God was to commit a crime. To
know such a girl is to respect for ever the nun's orders in which
natures like hers take refuge.

" Josephte, ma'amselle," said Chrysler very quietly and pleadingly,
" do you not love François ? "

The blood swept over her forehead again, and changed it once
more from white to red. The tears stopped in her eyes and she
regarded him for a moment with an intense look.

" François loves you," he proceeded.

He went on : " Where is the difficulty ? Is it not very cruel
to deny François your love ? Who made you promise that ? "

" O sir, they willed that I should marry another."

" It is only your father who wished you to marry Cuiller."

" Madame la Seigneuresse wished me to enter the convent."
Again she burst into bitter tears. Rocking to and fro she continued with breaking heart, " I promised it to God himself."

Chrysler had no wish to meddle with the belief of his new friends.
Here, however, it was a matter of humanity and common sense. He
could not let the young girl's life be ruined. He said : " My child,
le bon Dieu never asks the unreasonable. Is not God kinder than
you; and will he demand of you and François what you would not
of another ?"

" Monsieur, is it possible that that is true ?" sobbed she, weeping
freer.

" Does not your heart say so ? " said he.

" I know not. It must be so. You speak like a priest."

" Think," he said, " and pray to Him about it, and hope a
little for François. He loves you. It would be so cruel to him
to lose you."

" Henri's voice broke joyously out of the shrubbery :—

> " Good at all times
> Is sweet bread,
> But specially when
> With sugar spread."

Chrysler moved away, and passing through the trees stood on
the bank, looking down on the beach and the sunny surface of the
River. He had helped to right one little matter anyway, in
Dormillière.

A guttural call in a low voice startled him,—a subdued longdrawn
" Hoioch !—hoioch !—hoioch !" followed by a few words of instruc-

tions rapidly uttered in what seemed a kind of patois—and on turning he saw below, along the shore at the left, the little figure of the Bonhomme rapidly pulling in one end of a net through the water, while the other end was managed by a younger fisherman attired as rudely and queerly. It needed a close glance to see that the second man was François, assisting his father. Together they suggested that strange caste—the fishers of the great river—a caste living in the midst of a civilization, yet as little of it as the gipsies—families handing down apart among themselves from generation to generation manners, customs, haunts, unique secrets of localities, and sometimes apparently a marvellous skill. These are the true geographers and unboasting Nimrods. You who have ever seen the strange sight of the spearing under the flame of immense torches in the rapids of the Buisson, where no straining of your own eyes could ever discern the trace of a fish ; and you with whom it was an article of faith that certain death waited in every channel, swirl and white horse of the thundering Lachine Rapids, until one day some one speculated how the market boats of the lake above could turn up every morning safe and regular at the Bonsecours Market,—will be ready to understand.

However, it was not long before the net was drawn up and Chrysler stood beside them, the greetings were over and all three were duly seated, each on his chosen boulder under the green poplar saplings, talking :

"François," said the Bonhomme to his son, "Monsieur does not think it probable that Cuiller will marry Josephte."

The young man's unconquerable cheerfulness faded for a moment. He was silent.

" Why is it Mr. Benoit will not accept you ?" Chrysler asked, very interested.

" Solely because I lost my money, sir. I was coming to receive his blessing on our wishes."

" How was the money lost ? That was a singular circumstance."

" I had seven hundred and fifty dollars in my pocket. It was on the steamboat down from Montreal, at night time, in the lower cabin. I got a corner with Cuiller between two barrels and a bale of blankets and went to sleep from time to time. The lamps did not burn well. There was a crowd of people. A pedlar was next me whose features I have forgotten. Cuiller says it was that pedlar who took my money. I will not blame a man without knowing something about him ; but the truth is that when I got up and searched my pockets, my purse, my money, my pleasure, my life's profit,—all were lost, and I had nothing for it but to sit down and cry tears, after enquiring of all the people."

" In what pieces was your money ?"

" Six bills of a hundred, ten tens and ten fives, sir !"

" Don't you recollect anything about the pedlar ?"

" I was certain I recollected him getting off, but Cuiller saw him later."

" If Cuiller knew he took your purse why did'nt he wake you or stop him ?"

" I don't know, sir."

" Cuiller is as much to blame as the pedlar."

" You think so ?" said the simple Bonhomme.

CHAPTER XXXVI.

ZOTIQUE'S MISGIVING.

At sunset of the day before the Election, Chamilly came over very tired from the Institution and ordered tea to be brought out on the lawn. Little Brebœuf sat with them; the visiting politicians also; and last, least, and highly delighted at the honor, Francois Vadeboncœur *dit* Le Brun. To-morrow is the election day.

"How do we stand, Zotique?" Chamilly asked, with some air of fatigue. Zotique's duty of directing the actual carrying out of the campaign made him an authority on the "feel" of the constituency.

"Brebœuf will give you figures," replied he, reticently, for the struggle had proved grave. The Curé had almost succeeded, so far, in keeping his vow.

"Eh bien, ma brebis?"

"From the lists as Zotique has marked them I compute a majority of 28."

"Morbleu,—that's not comfortable!" exclaimed a young editor, fond of old oaths.

"But these estimations of Mr. Genest's prove surprisingly accurate," explained Chamilly.

"A majority of 28, composed as follows:" Brebœuf continued; "Dormillière, 83 to 44—majority 39; Petite Argentenaye, 96 to 47:—majority 49; St. Dominique, 11 to 19—majority 8; Miséricorde, majority 47. *Esneval.—*"

"Wait!"

Zotique spoke, and his eyes darkened energetically.

"I cannot guarantee you, Miséricorde."

All looked at each other. There was consternation.

"But surely Benoit has reported on that place," said Chamilly.

"In my absence. He has met me as little as possible. But Cuiller was seen an hour ago *entering the Circuit Court.*"

"Traitors!" breathed de la Lande.

"I do not trust this American. Unless I was ever mistaken, he and Benoit are goods and effects of Libergent, and we must save Miséricorde without letting those know, or perish. Let one go over; you cannot, and I cannot, nor any of the prominent, but let us send our François here, let him discover how it stands, and be back within two hours, so that we can work there, if needful, the rest of the night. This is the only salvation."

"I will go," cried François cheerfully, and picking up his hat, started rapidly away. Josephte came in at the gates as he was passing out; she bowed to him, and moved by us into the house, wrapped in the composure of one mourning at heart.

On hurried François, blithely unconscious of any dark prospect on his hopes of Josephte, but in visions, as he walked, of a little snow-white cottage known to him, with only one window in front, green-shuttered, but a dear little opening in the attic gable, and a leafy honey suckle creeping over the door way.

CHAPTER XXXVII.

A CRIME!

"The veil of mist that held her eyes was rent
As by a lightning flash......"

—W. KIRBY.

An hour passes. The shades draw on and begin to blend hues and forms. Chrysler moves his deliberative survey over the neat-clipped grass and the tall hedge, the poplars looking over it from the other side of the highway, the boughs and trunks of the great triple tree— and the little pinnacles along the Manor-house. A couple of the visitors along the paths are discussing the situation with dapper Parisian steps and gestures.

Suddenly the shades creep perceptibly deeper. The gate rattles. A wild acting man—it is Benoit in his sky-blue clothes—rushes panting in, throwing out his arms before him, stumbling and gasping inarticulately lamentations of anguish. "He is dead; my God, the poor young man! Poor François! My God! my God!"

Yes, it is Benoit Iscariotes.

Everyone springs to him. A great tragedy has occurred—for Dormillière; perhaps little for a more experienced world. In Benoit's mind quivers a scene that has set shouting all the wild voices of his conscience. Ever-cheerful François, so full of life, so faithful, well named "Vadeboncœur," lies motionless upon the highway, deadly white, with glazed, half-closed eyes. Blood trickles from his open mouth, scatters from a frightful gash over his forehead, and bathes the ground in a dark pool; and a heavy stone lies near and relates its murderous tale. This is what guilty Jean Benoit saw at his feet, as, having finished his "labors" to his own satisfaction he was returning from Miséricorde in the footsteps of his coadjutor Cuiller. O, as the poor body lay in the blood like a judgment before him, and those half-closed eyes seemed to gleam at him from their lids, what a fearful blow did Conscience strike that hypocrite, leaping from the lair in which it had long lain in wait!

He cannot stir. A mighty thunder cloud rises up from behind high above him, and darkens the earth. A silence lies on the trees, the road, the moor, and all around to the horizon—a silence accusing him.

Not a leaf moved. The sun went down. The bright little narrow gleam under the eyelids of the dead stared slily up to him with an awful triumph. His heart was caught by the grip of a skeleton hand. He could feel its several sinews as they tightened their grasp. It was impossible to break away—the grip of the hand was on the heart in his breast, and he was in the power of the triumphant *corpse !*

What made him reel, what made him leap at length with such an insane cry, over the ghastly obstacle? He will go mad. This not quite balanced brain might coldly enough commit even some kinds of murder, but fright can unhinge it. Is he not mad, to flee so wildly? He runs—he runs—he gropes, under his black thundercloud and load of fright and agony, towards the glimmer that he must fly to those he has wronged. To her first—to Josephte, his cruelly-treated daughter—the hour tells him where she is! Flying, stumbling, pained, groaning, out of breath, fearing the lone hedges of the road, in wild struggle throwing his vain lust of appearances for once to the winds, and having behind and above him as he fled, the sky filled with vast pursuing shapes, with shrieks and curses, and before all the pursuers the course, he reaches at last the Manoir, and stops before it crying out.   It seems as if the instinct failed him here, and the Mansion's imposing front forbade.

She hears though.   The maiden's heart, amid the world's indefinite voices, beats sharply at certain sounds before the ear has caught them, for they strike the inner strings of its being.   First a pang of great alarm,—and then she heard.   Rushing forth, she clasps the sobbing wretch in her arms and cries, " My father, what say'st thou !   My God, what is it ?—what has befallen François ? —O my dear father !"

" He is dead, he is dead !—thy loved one,—at La Miséricorde."

" O Holy Virgin !"

Josephte did not fall in a swoon : she darted towards the gate.

Chrysler took the man and made him sit down on a bench,—a wild spectacle of reason in the course of dethronement.   The household stood about : the two visitors looked on curiously and made useless suggestions.   Haviland and Zotique, driving past to make sure of Miséricorde, heard a commotion and turned their horses in.   Benoit threw himself on his knees to Chamilly, violently begging his forgiveness, and incoherently confessing the evil work of himself and Spoon, whereat Zotique attacked him with maledictions.

Chamilly restrained his companion.   Soul of man was never seen to soar more easily over injury.

" My dear friend, calm yourself.   If there has been bad work, what should be done now is to try and rectify it.   Repeat what you were saying of François."

" The poor young man !   The poor young man !   I have seen him dead on the road."

The impulse to act was that which came naturally to Haviland. " Not a moment, Zotique !" and almost immediately the rattle of the wheels was dying into the distance.

CHAPTER XXXVIII.

THE PASSING OF THE HOST.

They found François, Chamilly said, with Josephte kneeling over him loosening his collar, and tenderly binding her neckerchief over his head with neatness and gentleness quite enough indeed for any Heaven-selected Sister of Charity.

Running home breathless, dishevelled and desperate, she had frightened her brother and grandfather into speechless activity by a terrible command to harness a horse! Dragging out a light vehicle herself she speedily completed the arrangements, and whipping the animal pitiless lashes, dashed out of the presence of her relatives and was soon at the side of her injured lover, on the moorland road.

It must not tell against Zotique's humanity that he had all this time such a mastering sense of the necessity of getting on to Miséricorde that, after barely aiding to place the body on Chamilly's vehicle, he took possession of the lighter one of Josephte, and sped on for his destination. The young girl and Haviland, however, conveyed their charge carefully and safely to the farm-house, had him laid upon her own prettily-belaced bed, and Haviland insisted—was it not a sacrifice in him on that critical evening of his election!—in watching with her the whole night by the bedside of François. As the silent hours were broken by the occasional sobs of Josephte, the young seigneur often gazed anxiously into the face of his faithful friend, wiping the bruised forehead and hoping that he might not die.

Chrysler hurried down into the village in the dusk for medicine. By the occasional lights of houses he discerned the people, up and out discussing the exciting topic. Shadowy young men were standing on the path, straining their eyes to make out who passed by ; shadowy fathers of families sat together at their doorways ; half discernible women conversed from window to window.

A hand-bell rings somewhere in the dark. It slowly swings and rings a thin, melancholy warning tone, comes nearer, a lantern appears, the young men, the fathers, the women, the miscellaneous groups, seem, for half-a-second, to disappear like lights put out, they drop on their knees so instantly wherever they happen to be. A white-robed figure—an acolyte—passes ; feebly shone upon by a lantern ; the "young curé" follows, bearing the holy wafer,—a ghostly procession ; and Chrysler takes off his hat, for he recognizes it as the passing of the Host.

When they are fairly past, and have disappeared into the gloom, the shadowy shapes all rise from their knees, and follow the direction with eyes and ears, and a distinct, ominous murmur passes through the whole village, for clearly François Le Brun is in *articulo mortis.*

CHAPTER XXXIX.

THE ELECTION.

Election day at Dormillière was as election days in country places always—that is, a great peal of driving to and fro, and a great deal of crowding about the doors of the poll, and a dense atmosphere of smoke and bad jokes among the few to whom the polling-room was reserved, and now and then a flying visit from Haviland, Libergent, or Grandmoulin, for either of whom the people immediately made way by stumbling back on each other's toes; and intermittent activity at head-quarters; and ominous quiet at the parsonage.

Zotique was mysterious, and in better humor. He supervised with determination, and seemed to know how to calculate the exact effect of everything. Brebœuf was marvellously transformed into a little flying. spider, running backwards and forwards strengthening Haviland's web. The Honorable seemed to act slowly, but really with deliberation and effect, remarking neglected points, and himself seeing that certain "weak ones" were brought to the right side of the poll. The schoolmaster was away haranguing the back parishes. For the Blue side, Picault and Grandmoulin appeared but once on the scene, but the energy of Ross de Bleury was astonishing. Cajoling, ordering, opening bottles aside and treating, volubly greeting everybody in his strong voice all day, he seemed to have raised supporters for his party of whom no one would have dreamt except Zotique;

but the little closet up in the attic satisfied the requirements of strict logic.

Haviland had added the fatigues of the last night to weeks of wearing labor, with consequences at length upon his fund of spirits, and also plainly on his face.   He felt, like Grandmoulin, that his battle was principally with De la Lande in the back of the county, cheering up his ranks.

About two o'clock Zotique drove over to Miséricorde alone.   He did not return for an hour and a half, and when he did, his expression had altered to one of decided triumph, though still mysterious and silent.   Zotique, in fact, the evening before, when he drove to Miséricorde in Josephte's little gig, found what he had suspected to be the truth, that Benoit and Spoon had bought every vote of the hamlet, and paid for them, in the interest of Libergent; but he still believed it possible,—Benoit being incapacitated, and Spoon, he felt sure, not likely to turn up—to bend this plastic material the other way with the same tool, and casting, therefore, aside all delicate distinctions, he succeeded, by a reasonable hour in the evening, in obtaining once more the adhesion of the *hotellier* and most of the population, giving—for he had no Government funds like his opponents—his own personal notes for the amounts, and enjoining on the tavern-keeper to have the whole of the suffrages polled early. This was all he could do, as it was impossible for him to be present on the morrow, or to delegate any other person of Haviland's circle. His remaining anxiety was removed, when, on driving over, his investigations proved that the arrangement had been fully completed.

De Bleury only got the news in the morning, and Picault, who immediately hurried over at his suggestion, found himself too late, and his carefully prepared representation that "promissory notes representing an immoral compact were invalid" was of no use, while his invitation of the crowd to 'whiskeyblanc' only produced useless

condolences. " *C'est dommage, monsieur.*   If we could have known."
He was not altogether displeased, however, to find what he considered
the inevitable hole in Chamilly's professions of purity, and meeting
the latter driving just outside the place, he wheeled his horse across
the road and compelled an interview.

"You think you can do without Picault!" he laughed frankly.

"Let me pass, sir!" said Haviland, unwilling to put up with any
nonsense.

"To take up the promissory notes of your friend?"

"Do you think sir, that I use your inventions?   Let me pass, I tell
you," and he rose with his whip.

"I have seen the cards, Haviland; take the game; let us be part-
ners; what is the use of dissembling in this extraordinary manner?"

A flash of the whip,—a leap of the two animals,—Picault careen-
ing into the ditch, and Chamilly flying into Miséricorde.

CHAPTER XL.

HAVILAND REFUSES.

"Nobleness still makes us proud."
—FREDERICK GEORGE SCOTT.

The election was Haviland's.

A great crowd gathered into Dormillière at the close of that long day, thickening and pouring in from the country around, and arriving by boats across the river, to hear the returns : and as Zotique read them in triumph from a chair at the door of the Circuit Court, and the issue, at first breathlessly uncertain, finally appeared, the cheering became frantic.   Chamilly himself came out to them, an incomprehensible, determined aspect on his face, and amid deafening hurrahs, was seized and hurried on their shoulders across the square to the crier's rostrum, where he stood up before them.

And then and there took place the most unheard of incident, the most remarkable outcome of Haviland's lofty character, of which there as yet was record.

His voice can be heard distinct and clear over a perfect hush. What does he say? tell me,—have we really caught it correctly? Fact unique in political history ; *he was refusing the election on account of the frauds !*

"Grandmoulin,"—was Picault's subsequent remark, "The young fool has courage.   What a deep game he is playing.   I tell you he has more talent than the whole of our side together except yourself— curse him."

" It demonstrates the unpracticality of his methods ! " said the burly Montreal politician to Zotique, with self-satisfied disgust.

" No," returned Zotique, firmly, " If we had followed his methods it would have been far better. But nothing can make up for lack of intelligence : *Sacré bleu*. I ought to have had a better head than to leave these people to such as Cuiller and Benoit ! "

Chamilly addressed firm words to the disappointed electorate : " I seek not my own cause, friends It is yours in which I do this thing and do you, too, give all for country's honor. Lose not heart. Work on, like iron figures, receiving blows without feeling them. Be we young in our strength and hope, as Truth our mistress is perennial. Accept from me who according to the rule of faint hearts ought to be most crushed by our failure, the motto, " *Encouraged* by disaster ! "

CHAPTER XLI.

FIAT JUSTITIA.

" I wonder at you!—I wonder at you!" exclaimed Chrysler, pacing the drawingroom of the Manor-house, to his friend, " What will be the result of it ?"

"Cher Monsieur," Haviland replied.   " I have done my duty and what have I to do with events ?   What is Dormillière county and a year or two of the consequences of this election ?   I do not live in them or of them."

The face of the far-seeing god himself, whose statue stood once more near, could scarcely show less regret than the easy, indomitable countenance of Chamilly ; yet that his nerves had been strained to a severe pitch, lines of exhaustion upon it clearly told, and his restless, reckless movements from one spot and position to another made his friend anxious.   A raw wind storm had risen quickly from the east and whistled without.   He advanced to the window and threw both its curtains wide apart, revealing under an obscured snatch of struggling moonlight, the heavens covered with rapid-moving clouds, and the poplars opposite bending their vague shapes beneath the wind,—the beginning of one of those storms which come up from the Gulf, and overrun the whole region for days.

" I should like to be on the River now," he remarked exultingly. Madame entered at the moment and heard him.

" Be quiet, Chamilly," chided the Seigneuresse.

" Alors, Alors," he said impatiently, as if casting about for something active to do, and left the room.

" Madame de Bois-Hebert," Chrysler said, " have you news from Mademoiselle Josephte ?"

" That young person," replied she, " has descended to the plane of her condition : I have no further interest in her."

But the devout lady sighed.

The Gulf storm lowered steadily and disagreeably all next day and the visitor saw nothing of Chamilly, who kept in his room until the evening. But there was one excitement which occupied everyone else's attention :

" Who do you think struck François ?" Chrysler said to Zotique at the Circuit Court House.

" The Bonhomme has tracked Spoon through every bush and bay on the coast, and has caught him getting aboard the steamboat at Petite Argentenaye," the Registrar replied.

A crowd came down the road. All the crowd were excited. They ran about a long waggon in which were on the first seat, the Honorable and Bonhomme ; on the second a constable and prisoner handcuffed. Spoon, who cowered like a captured wild beast ready to whine with fright, was clapped into a private room and a stray Bleu flew off for Libergent to act as advocate. The crowd, soon uncomfortably larger, diverted itself by taking oratorical views of his guilt or innocence : but the prevailing opinion of the prisoner personally was expressed by one in an unfastidious proverb : " Grosse crache, grosse canaille."

Libergent, accompanied by De Bleury, came over at once, for he had a good deal at stake in seeing that Spoon's trial should lead to no unpleasant revelations or consequences to the party. Closeted not more than half an hour he came out and said publicly to l'Honorable, who took seat as Magistrate upon the Bench under the great lion-and-unicorn painting. " My client makes option of opening the investigation at once. He is not guilty of the charge and can clear himself."

The Bonhomme cried excitedly,—" It's false ! "   His wife joined him with a wild scream of disappointment.   A murmuring ran about. "Silence ! " shouted the constable.

Every one involuntarily obeyed ; and Chrysler absorbed himself examining the articles taken from the prisoner's person.

The evidence was as soon disposed of as Libergent could have wished. Josephte gave her testimony to the appearance and surroundings of the injured man as she had found him.   She could relate no circumstances that pointed to Spoon.   The Bonhomme eagerly proffered his evidence.   It was torn to tatters by the advocate : he had nothing to tell but rambling suspicions, and was told to stand down.   It was discovered that none in fact had anything pertinent to say.   Benoit was mad ; François, unconscious ; and Libergent triumphantly asked for the prisoner's immediate discharge.

The great doubt on the part of justice was, clearly, why did the prisoner disappear ? But this was quickly resolved by witnesses who swore that Cuiller was entrusted with secret political business which necessitated absences and journeys in different parts of the country, and this, in the state of political affairs, was an obvious enough excuse.

Libergent pressed once again for the discharge.

"I must grant it," simply pronounced Mr. Genest.

Another scream pierced their ears   " Justice, oh God ; " the old wife of Le Brun shrieked in trembling syllables.   "They kill without hanging.   I demand JUSTICE !   Hear me, great God ! " and her bent frame and wrinkled face writhed pitiably.

But it was done.   Spoon descended with a sudden, wild grin and found himself free.   " In a few hours," he probably thought obscurely, " I can be far on my road."

" Pardon me," said Chrysler, however, standing up, to the surprise of everybody.   " Your Honor, I have another charge to bring against the prisoner, and I ask his re-arrest."

The Honorable made a sign to the constable to stay Cuiller.

" These bills," Chrysler said, holding out the bank notes which were found in the purse of Spoon, " are marked with the initials of François Le Brun's name. I am ready to charge the prisoner with having committed a larceny of money from François Le Brun on his journey from Montreal. I sustain it by these initials at the corners of bills just found on the prisoner's person. I am informed—"

" I object, your Honor," fairly shouted Libergent—" I object to any hearsay."

" What can you swear to of your own knowledge ?" asked l'Honorable of Chrysler, gently.

" To seeing these marks—"

" Which might be anything ! " snapped Libergent.

" To hearing—"

" No hearsay, sir ! "

" To having a conviction—"

" Upon no grounds whatever !—Your Honor, I press my just application for an immediate discharge."

" I cannot see that there is yet evidence enough," l'Honorable said courteously. " There are two charges, but both of them seem founded on vague suspicions which I cannot consider sufficient to detain the prisoner."

Libergent triumphantly glanced from Spoon to the audience.

At that moment, however, the man at his side rose up :—Ross de Bleury !

" If what Monsieur says is true," he exclaimed to the Honorable, throwing out his clenched hand,—" if these letters are found upon those notes, then I understand it. I can prove that this infernal, greasy, treacherous devil,—be he friend or traitor, or whatever he chooses to be, to the Bleu party or myself,—committed that despicable larceny and has wronged that poor young man. I was on the steamboat. I saw it. I saw him do it to his friend. Talking to the purser, I saw the act, but could not believe it a reality. On the parole of all my ancestors, I would never go back on a common thief, I would keep faith inviolate with a parricide, I have a secret sympathy with every brigand, but I have no place out of *l'enfer* itself for a traitor, *Dieu merci*.

" Swear the informant," said the Magistrate.

The picture at this instant of the frightened face of Spoon who collapsed into a seat by the Bar, of the excitement of the crowd, which had been gradually brought to a climax, the disgust of Libergent, relief of Chrysler, satisfaction of the little Bonhomme and his ,wife, the cynical roll of Zotique's eyes round the room, and serene, judicial face of the Honorable on the bench above, would have made the reputation of the greatest painter in Paris.

Afer all, Spoon was remanded for trial, and in due time, the Queen's Bench Court condemned him to the fullest penalty of the law for his murderous assault and larceny.

François meanwhile recovered, and was taken, pale and weak, but indescribably happy, in a carriage one morning beside Josephte to church, where the young Curé made her his faithful bride.

As for Benoit, " *il est tout en campagne*," they said. In less expressive terms, " his mind was hopelessly wandering."

* * * * *

To return to our current day however ; in the evening Chamilly came into the drawing room with some more manuscript, which he handed to Chrysler.

" Here is the rest of the story I have been writing," said he, " take it sir, and may it amuse you a little ; it is the key to the rest. I am going out on the River." And he went out of the Manoir door into the storm.

The manuscript proceeded as follows :

BOOK III.

BOOK OF ENTHUSIASMS (CONTINUED.)

BOOK III.

CHAPTER XLII.

QUINET'S CONTRIBUTION.

"O, skyward-looking, fleet-winged soul,
Earth hath no name for thine ideal flower!"
— MARY MORGAN.

For a night and a day after my talk with my father, I was a fool. Swelling names of ancestors rang proudly in my ears, and I shudder to think how easily I might have ended in a genealogist.

" Salut, Milord de Quinet."

" Bon soir, Chamilly," replied he, soberly.

"Aha, thou melancholy friend, the liver again, eh ? "

We were strolling along the half illuminated Grosvenor street under the elms. The dim, substantial mansions in their grounds and trees, pleased my foreign eyes and I was glad to find the city of Alexandra able to vie with the great cities of the world, and I thought of her as near, and for the moment, could not understand the humor of Quinet.

" You don't seem to know," said he, " at least, I thought I would tell you—that Miss Grant has gone away,"—he stopped and looked at me earnestly. —" I sympathise with you."

"Away !" I caught my breath. My spirits sank with disappointment. Alas ! Heaven seemed to ordain that my passion for her should never become a close communion, but only keep this light, ethereal touch upon me.

And so Quinet knew. "I do not ask you how : evidently you have known it all along ?" (It was the first time I had been spoken to

about my love for her, and it made me feel peculiarly.)   "Mon ami,
Quinet, tu es heureux ne pas aimer.   Que penses tu de ma chère ?"

"Go on, my friend Chamilly ; be steadfast, for thou could'st not
have chosen a sweeter, lovelier, holier divinity.   O my friend, be
steadfast and be happy.   Yes, as thou hast said, I have known this."

Quinet was diverting our steps along up-leading streets which
tended towards the Mountain, and soon we reached the head of one,
where a wall met us.

"This way," he said, striking aside into a field which formed part
of the Park.   "Adieu, civilization of street lights !" and he pressed
up into a dark grove where I stumbled after, and next, under the twilight of a sky full of stars, could descry dim outlines of the surroundings of our path and even of the Mountain, silent above us like a huge
black ghost.   We toiled up the steep stair, guiding ourselves by feeling, and in a few minutes were at Prospect Point, that jutting bit of
turf on the precipice's edge where the trees draw back and allow in
daytime a wide view of the city and surrounding country, and we
both stood breathless there in the dimness, in front of a sight bewilder-
ingly grand enough to of itself take one's breath away.

Above were the radiant constellations.   Below, between a belt of
weird horizon and the dark abyss at our feet, the city shone, its dense
blackness mapped out in stars as brilliant and myriad-seeming as
those overhead,—a Night above, a Night below !   Once before had I
looked from that crag upon Montreal, in a memorable sunset hour,
and remembered my impression of its beauty.   Below, the scarped
rock fell : the tops of trees which grew up the steep face lost themselves, lower, in a mass of grove that flourished far out, and besieged
the town in swollen battalions and columns of foliage.   Half over-
whelmed by this friendly assault, the City sat in her robes of grey and
red, proud mistress of half a continent, noble in situation as in
destiny.   A hundred spires and domes pointed up, from streets full

of quaint names of saints and deeds of heroes. The pinnacled towers of Notre Dame rose impressively in the distance. Past ran the glorious St. Lawrence, with its lovely islands of St. Helen's and the Nuns'.

Now, however, it seemed no longer a place upon earth at all. It was a living spirit. Quiet as the sky itself, its bright eyes looked far upward, and it was communing, in the loveliness of Nature, with the constellations.

" This is Life !" cried Quinet, who had hitherto been excited with suppressed feeling. " The vast winds come in to us from Ether. Night hides all that is common, and sprinkles the dark-blue vault with gold-dust ; the planets gleam far and pure amidst it, and Space sings his awful solo.

" All is one mighty Being. There he moves, the Great Creature, his crystal boundlessness encompassing his countless shapes. He faces us from every point. His God-soul looks through to us. He rises at our feet. He surrounds us in ourselves ; speaks and lives in us. Is he not resplendent, wondrous !

" We are out of the world of vain phantoms, Chamilly ! We are above the chatter of a wretched spot, a narrow life. Down there, nothing is not ridiculed that is not some phase of a provinciality. The dances in certain houses, the faces of some conceited club, long-spun names, business or gossip, or to drive a double carriage, are the gaslight boundaries of existence ! Pah ! it is a courtyard, bounded by four square walls, a path or two to walk in, and the eyes of busy-bodies to order our doings and sneer us out of our souls. How they deny us that the centre of the systems is immeasurably off there in Pleiades ! What fools we are. We follow trifles we value at the valuation of idiots ; we cherish mean ideas ; we believe contracted doctrines ; we do things we are ashamed of ; dropping at last like the animals, with alarm that we die.

" Look off into the heart of It! the heart of It! beyond there !" he exclaimed, stretching his arm. " Forget our courtyard ! Nay, returning there, let us remember that this infinite ocean is above it —a boundless sea beneath and around, an unknown universe within. Take in this scene and feel the rich thrills of its majesty stir you. You are of it; you came out of it ; it is your mother, father, lover ; it will never let you die ; that heart of it to which your utmost straining cannot pierce, was once and will again be known to you. Its beauty caresses your soul from another world, and it is Love Divine which moves those stars.* Your own sweet passion, Chamilly, is the child of that divine Love, and in it you mount towards the heavens, and yearn as by inspiration, for a mysterious ideal existence? The poets and romancers lightly say of it "a divine power:" they think they say a metaphor—a lie; but I tell you it is true ! May it assist you to live the life of the universe."

"Each man," he cried, "who pursues his highest is a prophet ! Ever there is an inward compulsion in our race to press on, and we hear the heroes of the front as they fall, crying " Forward, forward, forward, forward, forward !"

While he spoke, for he said much besides, many of the lights were disappearing, we seemed to be being left alone, and the church-towers of the city chorussed the hour of ten.

---

*Dante—Divina Commedia.

CHAPTER XLIII.

HAVILAND'S PRINCIPLE.

The final step in the progression of influences was, strange to say, a dream.   Our residence was then on Grosvenor street,—a Florid Gothic one after the model of Desdemona's House in Venice.   My own little room was fitted up in a Moorish fashion.

After the scene with Quinet on Prospect Point, I sat up till a late hour, for I found a letter from Grace, telling jocularly of their journey just commenced in the delightful Old World, and seriously of Alexandra's ambitions.   I sat thinking with my arms folded on the table till I fell asleep.   Then I felt at first that I was lifted up on the Mountain again, and leaving that presently, was carried out into space far away among the stars.   Phosphorescent mists and cloud masses passed over the region, and among these appeared various figures, the last of which was that of a certain old Professor of ours.

The most apparently dissimilar things come to us in dreams.   A lecture of the Professor's had once greatly impressed me : " Conscience is Reason," he said.   "To do a right thing is to do simply the reasonable thing ; to do wrong is to do what is unreasonable.—

" Now think," he said, " what this means."

What could such words have to do with a dream ?

" What is Duty ?" he proceeded, " Whence the conviction, the mysterious fact, that whatever my inclination may be, I *ought* to do some act—ought to do it though the cup of pleasure be dashed from the lifting hand, though a loved face must pale, though the stars in their high courses reel, and the gulfs of perdition smoke,—why is it that the grave, unalterable 'Ought' must still demand reverence?"

His voice rose.

" Immanuel Kant !"

The familiar name caught my ear, and I attended.

" To him Heaven gave it to solve the problem. Think what Reason is ! Be men for once and attend to one deep matter ! Think what Reason is !—the divinest part of us, and common with the Divine, as with every Intelligence ; speaking not of the voice of the individual, but one sound everywhere to all. It is more truth than metaphor to name it the VOICE OF GOD."

In my dream, the Professor repeated, as if with mystic significance, the cry : "Conscience is Reason !" and as these words vaguely reached me, his figure dissolved into a rolling cloud, which grew at once into a shape of giant form, and addressed me in echoing tones : "The unalterable Ought ! the unalterable Ought !" reverberating from the depths and heights.

I awoke at the sound, and collecting my energies—for I had been half-asleep,—stretched out my hand to my note-book, looked up the lecture, and with the words swaying before me, read sleepily :—

" Leave us Reason in any existence ;—strip us of sight, sound, touch, and all the external constitution of nature, clothe us with whatever feelings and powers, place us in whatever scenes may come— but gift us with this universal faculty, our power of knowing truth. Otherwise, with rudder lost, we are dreamers on a drifting wreck, and where were the Divine One, and this harmonious architecture of the universe, and all things trustworthy, proportioned, eternal, exalting ?

" Leave us Reason, and, children of God, we may from any point start out to see Our Father, His voice indicating from within the paths to Him which somewhere surely lie near to every- where. Leave us Reason, and, brothers of men, we recognize that each Intelligence is of value equal to ourselves, and more precious than aught else can be, and we perceive the due relations of an orderly world.

"The voice within in simple dignity commands "—

But the lines swam before me : I could not hold my head up : the Moorish room expanded to the height and magnificence of a Hall of Magic, the dream of starry space returned and the pure lights circled in it singing to me in chorus. Space itself seemed to become the veiled countenance of a Mysterious Power, which "half-revealed and half-concealed" itself on every hand, and out of the midst of a dark-blue sky, appeared the form and face of Alexandra, like a Princess-Madonna, smiling, O so earnestly and kindly.

I started, and woke again. The Professor's notes were still under my eyes, and I read the words, " Lose yourself and live as if you were one of the others. Exalted on this pinnacle you are prepared for any existence ; you have learnt your path through eternity, and the world and its vicissitudes may sweep by you like winds past a statue."

As I slowly thought over all the dream, and comprehended its remarkable character, I conceived it as a revelation.

"The highest things,—I have found them at last !" I exultantly cried, in a final enthusiasm—"the total subjection of self and obedience of the whole life to Reason ! What shall I care more for events and opinions, or any matter that but concerns myself and a fleeting world ! I will seek in my actions ever the greater, finer, nobler thing for all, and the rule will be aim sufficient !"

"I saw that DUTY is the Secret of the World."

It was only a question to choose my largest, finest, noblest field of work for all. Difficulties disappeared, and the great aim soon appeared before me of the cultivation of the national spirit.

The nation must found and shape its own work on the same deep idea.

CHAPTER XLIV.

DAUGHTER OF THE GODS.

"Soft was the breath of balmy spring
In that fair month of May."

—GEO. MURRAY.

Time flew brightly for some days, as an early spring, having poured its thousand rivulets out of the melting snows, began to dry the soil and instil into the willows and birches the essences that soon cover them with refreshing green, and earth suddenly teems with leafing and flying life, with odor of buds and laughing variety of shade and sun.

I, as is my nature, was deeply under the spell.

" Rossignolet du bois joli,
Emporte-moi-t-une lettre !"

Alexandra was coming home !

St. Helen's Island, named affectionately by Champlain after his fair young wife, Hélène, stretches its half-mile of park along the middle of the River opposite the city of Montreal. It is at all times a graceful sight; in summer by the refreshing shade of its deep groves beheld from the dusty city ; in winter by the contrast of its flowing purple crest of trees with the flat white expanse of ice-covered river. The lower end, towards which the outlines of its double hill tend, is varied by the walls and flagstaffs of a military establishment, comprising some grey barracks, a row of officers' quarters, and a block-house, higher on the hill. In former times, when British redcoats were stationed here, and military society made the dashing feature in fashionable life, when gay and·high-born parties scattered their laughter through the trim groves, improved and kept in shape by labor of the rank and file, and "the Fusileers and the Grenadiers" marched in or out with band and famous colors flying, and the regimental goat or dog, and shooting practice, officers' cricket and football matches, and mess dinners, kept the island lively and picturesque, St. Helen's was a theatre of unceasing charm to the citizens.

"Is she here yet?" I asked, eagerly grasping the hand of Grace, who, more exceedingly pretty than ever, had invited all their friends to meet them on the island, in the grove, "I am delighted to see you back. It is almost worth the absence."

"And I welcome you as Noah the dove, after the waste of waters," exclaimed she, laughing. "But I must answer your first question before it is repeated. No, *mon frère*, I am afraid she is not to be here to day. She is a little ill with fatigue."

"O my poor friend!" I exclaimed, and led Grace down the avenue of leafing trees in which we were; for this grove had been planted in regular walks by the garrison forty years before, and the turf had been sown with grass that sprang up at that season a vivid green. The dell had been a theatre of the gaieties of days past. To me it was deserted loveliness—a scene prepared and not occupied.

"Is she very ill?"

"No; merely tired. You see she is a thousand times more industrious than I. Nothing could content her over there unless she was putting out her utmost. She said it was her ambition to improve, like the great men and women; that she was strong and ought to make up for some of her imperfections by greater diligence. I never saw anyone so anxious to do a thing perfectly. The great Bertini in Florence said of her—'She will certainly be greater than Angelica Kauffmann.'. . .'Alexandra,' he said, 'will rank with men.' The egotism of the creature! You see there are others who admire her besides yourself."

"None more passionately."

"I thought so.—But look this way, Tityrus," said she, wheeling quickly and stepping forward. "How do you do, Alexandra!"

There she stood, pale and ill, but proud of carriage as ever.

"So you came after all? Here is Mr. Haviland, gladder even than I to see you!"

I saw Grace, in a moment, the duties of hostess being temporarily undertaken by Annie, walking down a path with soldierly Lockhart Mackenzie, who had come over from the "quarters" in his uniform.

Alexandra and I found ourselves wandering into the wood and climbing the hillside at the loftiest point of the Island, where, on the summit, the trees permitted us a wide view of the St. Lawrence, its islands and ships and the open country ; while the afternoon sunlight fell brokenly upon the faint colors of her face and her golden hair.

"Do you admire distant landscapes?" I asked constrainedly.

"They remind me of high aims and the broad views of great minds," returned she, looking outward.

"You favor aiming high," I said, "I always thought so of you."

She turned her glance for a moment to me, and asked seriously : "How can people aim low? Do you know the lines of Goëthe :"

> "Thou must either strive and rise,
> Or thou must sink and die."

Daughter of the immortals!

"I wonder what you will say of *my* aims," I stammered.

"May you tell them? I should like very much to hear." And as she seemed to bend from a queen into a womanly companion, I noticed my gift, the brooch of Roman mosaic, on her breast.

While she listened, for I told her fully the story of my quest for the highest things, its strange solution, and my present purposes, I was surprised to discover that her intelligence was master

of the whole without effort. "O, I have often talked philosophy with
Mr. Quinet," she explained. Her spiritual eyes glistened with profound beautiful depths as she looked down into the forest-shades
before us. A color had suffused itself over her face so lovely that
the glorified creature beside me seemed to surpass my intensest
ideal.

"It *is* the Voice of the Universe," she said, and her cheeks
flushed, "I once heard the Spirit of All, called, 'Heart of
Heaven, Heart of Earth,' and I added 'Heart of Man.' Obey
it, obey your best thoughts." She looked at me with such a glance
of sacred sympathy, that—O joy, the first words filling life with
fragrance have been spoken!

*   *   *   *   *

It was short, our sweet bridal and few days of united life, and of
bliss at the old château d'Esneval. Gravely ill,—worse,—recovering,
—then DEAD. O God, was it possible?

Yes; I saw her lying amid garlands of evergreens and white robes,
in a low-lighted chamber of the château, still and transfigured into a
changed, unearthly beauty, the alas! so thin lips lightly parted in
a smile, the abundant golden hair I used to admire brushed neatly
away from her forehead, the darkened eyelids that told of long
exhaustion peacefully closed as if on visions of heaven—as if she saw
God, being pure in heart. Supernaturally lovely as her soul had
been through life the wearied sufferer lay in death, white tuberoses
pressing her poor thin cheek—one purity affectionate to another.
Ah, it was a vision. I never saw one on whom Heaven loved so
constantly to breathe sweetness. Neither health could roughen her
beauty nor sickness' drive it away : for the soul, after all, will shine
through the body, will lift it up, and if glorious will leave it worthy
of itself.

*   *   *   *   *

Alas, ungovernable, passionate grief! Alas the sight of heart-broken friends and painful rites of burial, the anguish of bereavement, the irresistible longing to die and be with her;—and Quinet's grief also; for then he had confessed that he had loved her too.

*   *   *   *   *

And now we who knew her recognise that she was sent into this world for a season, and tenderly watched and favored of heaven for high purposes—for the stirring example and strong influence of a short but lofty life.

In moments of weakness the irresistible longing to go to her returns upon me, but it is she whose Athênê vision impels to throw it off, to stand ground firmly and push forward with determination towards the years which must be endured, and the glorious work which calls to be achieved. Canada, beloved, thy cause is led by an angel!

*   *   *   *   *

What of Quinet? Noble friend, when I gave way unlike a man (though that is with God, who knows how much hearts can bear); he it was who held his own despair sternly back and put out efforts to solace and quiet mine. In these years he has grown stronger, but become ascetic towards the outer world—an Ishmaelite who cares not to own himself a son of Abraham, but lives wild in the deserts of philosophy on locusts and wild honey. He will never marry, but has devoted himself to the problems of the Secret of the World, in which he too believes, though his studies have led him far more scientifically than me; and yet in his hours of thought, I know that a vision of beauty and a sweet voice will often startle him, and he rises then into scenes of his loftiest, grandest life.

O, Alexandra! Alexandra!

CONCLUSION OF CHAMILLY HAVILAND'S NARRATIVE.

CHAPTER XLV.

NOT THE END.

"Requiem æternam dona eis, Domine, et lux perpetua luceat eis."

—Ps. cxiv.

When Chrysler came to this sad close of the story, he woke from his absorption in the manuscript and became conscious of the surroundings. The late hour, the strange place, even the silent-burning candles, and above all the shock of grief for Chamilly at his great bereavement, oppressed him into deep loneliness. The wind dashed gusts of rain against the casement and shook it savagely. He thought of the storm and blackness without—how the tempest must be hounding the black waves—the wolfish ferocity of their onward rushes— the dread battle any mortal would fight who found himself among them on a night like this.

Is Chamilly safe at home again ?

Of course, at this hour.

What an unusual fellow. How strange to enjoy such beating rain, such blinding darkness and fierce contest of strength with nature ! How fearless ! How few like him in this or any virtue ! Did there in fact exist another his equal ?

No ; Haviland stood alone—the climax of a race.

As Chrysler pondered, dull sounds reached him, breaking in on these meditations. A door opened below, and heavy feet tramped in. Voices, and then cries of alarm, and then lamentations of all the household startled him. Steps sounded coming up the stairs, and a man's sob, and then a gentle knock.

"Open!" Chrysler responded.

· Pierre entered, the picture of woe, and broke down: "O monseigneur Monseigneur Chamilly is dead."

They had found his boat and his body, washed ashore.

The windows of the Parish Church were darkened with thick black curtains, the altar was heavily draped, the strains of the mournful Mass of the Dead swayed to the responses of a sorrowing people. In the midst, raised upon a lofty catafalque whose sable drapery was surrounded with a starry maze of candle-lights, lay the silent remains of Chamilly Haviland, who loved Canada. Pure and earnest in life, he receives his reward in the world of her he loved, who went before him.

A tablet among those of his fathers, facing the Seigniorial pew, recorded, for a little, the name of the last d'Argentenaye; but now the proud Curé at length has had his will, and instead of its venerable house of God, Dormillière wears in its centre a pretentious nondescript structure of cut-stone.

Chrysler has done what he could to repair the country's loss by raising his voice with rejuvenated energy in support of good will and progress, in the Legislative halls.

"L'ideé Canadienne too," Quinet asserts with hope and fire, in his seer-like editorials, "is not lost; it is founded on the deepest basis of existence : on the simplicity of common sense ; on the true affections, the true aspirations of the people, on righteousness, on love of, God, on DESTINY !"

THE END.